Ghost Mikawa

Illustration by
necömi

Looks ARE ALL YOU NEED

▶ 1. Shiika's Crescendo

"I'll just leave all that stuff up to you, Gak. As long as I can hear some nice sounds, I'll be satisfied."

Seeker

Ultimate Wannabe
Mana Akihabara

Genius Vsinger Seeker
Shiika Ikebukuro

LOOKS ARE ALL YOU NEED

1. Shiika's Crescendo

Ghost Mikawa

Illustration by:
necömi

YEN ON
New York

LOOKS ARE ALL YOU NEED

(M) **Ghost Mikawa**

Illustration by:
(N) **necömi**

Translation by: **Evie Lund**

(▶) 1. Shiika's Crescendo

KAOSAE YOKEREBA IIKYOSHITSU Vol. 1 SHIIKA CRESCENDO
©Ghost Mikawa, necömi 2022
First published in Japan in 2022 by KADOKAWA CORPORATION, Tokyo.
English translation rights arranged with KADOKAWA CORPORATION, Tokyo through TUTTLE-MORI AGENCY, INC., Tokyo.

Yen On
150 West 30th Street, 19th Floor
New York, NY 10001

Visit us at yenpress.com
facebook.com/yenpress
twitter.com/yenpress
yenpress.tumblr.com
instagram.com/yenpress

First Yen On Edition: August 2023
Edited by Yen On Editorial: Shella Wu, Leilah Labossiere
Designed by Yen Press Design: Jane Sohn, Wendy Chan

Yen On is an imprint of Yen Press, LLC.
The Yen On name and logo are trademarks of Yen Press, LLC.

The publisher is not responsible for websites (or their content) that are not owned by the publisher.

Library of Congress Cataloging-in-Publication Data
Names: Mikawa, Ghost, author. | necömi, illustrator. | Lund, Evie, translator.
Title: Looks are all you need / Ghost Mikawa ; illustration by necömi ; translation by Evie Lund.
Other titles: Kaosae yokereba iikyoshitsu. English
Description: First Yen On edition. | New York : Yen On, 2023- |
Identifiers: LCCN 2023016566 | ISBN 9781975371258 (v. 1 ; trade paperback)
Subjects: LCGFT: Light novels.
Classification: LCC PZ7.1.M5537 Lo 2023 | DDC [Fic]—dc23
LC record available at https://lccn.loc.gov/2023016566

ISBNs: 978-1-9753-7125-8 (paperback)
       978-1-9753-7126-5 (ebook)

10 9 8 7 6 5 4 3 2 1

LSC-C

Printed in the United States of America

CONTENTS

EVERYONE HAS TALENT.
IF ONLY WE COULD REALIZE IT.

Chapter 0:
Let's Begin by Introducing the Main Character

Judging people based on looks is totally outdated, if you ask any opinionated adult living in 2020.

Think of all those posts on social media where people claim to have found happiness and fulfilment regardless of their appearance. Think of those street interviews where every single interviewee says the same thing: Personality matters so much more than looks.

They're not saying it just to appear cool. To them, they really believe it's true. That's just reality. Actually, these days, when it comes to finding someone to date, it's pretty common not to fuss too much over a handsome or pretty face.

Instead, we log in to the popular battle royale FPS online game *EPEX* and meet someone on there. We DM the other person and start to get to know each other a little better... That's how it goes in the world of those who've grown up in the digital age. Dating apps? Those are for the scammers.

Still, at the tender age of eighteen, I, Gakuto Ikebukuro, adrift in the midst of such an era, simply can't believe the words of the self-proclaimed It's What's Inside That Counts brigade.

I mean, hear me out.

"You people... Your profile pics show only handsome guys and pretty girls..."

Selfies. Anime-style drawings. It's clear that whichever one they go for, they're just trying to present themselves as someone "cool."

They want to be seen as cool by other people. And of course they want that.

Fools, all of 'em, I thought, narrowing my eyes at the hot male player (or their avatar) before me and using all the 9 mm Parabellum bullets in my arsenal to shoot them in the face.

As the victory text flashed on the screen, I unmuted my Wizcode (an app that lets you voice chat with other players) and congratulated my ally on a good fight well fought.

"That was a splendid shot there at the end, Gaku-Gaku."

"Thank you very much, Zeke."

"Seems like they're some hot name streamer, but they logged off, red-faced, the second they lost. The youth these days don't know online etiquette."

"They have zero shame."

"Truly quite shameless."

Gaku-Gaku was my online name. Gakuto Ikebukuro becomes Gaku-Gaku. An appropriate name.

I was chatting with Zeke, my friend in the world of online games. All I knew about him was that his voice was deep and cool—and that he worked with computers.

He had this old-fashioned way of speaking that seemed to be influenced by some anime character or other, and I thought it was a little weird. But if you just considered it part of his personality, it wasn't anything important to get hung up on.

"Incidentally, have you heard it yet? Seeker's new I Tried Singing… video? It was uploaded the day before yesterday."

"You mean 'Laughter at the Bottom of the Ocean'?"

"Indeed, indeed."

Zeke laughed, clearly in a good mood.

"It is, truly, a delight for the ears, the juxtaposition of those soothing, deep-ocean-sinking sounds and that crystal clear singing voice. I have been having a terrible bout of insomnia as of late, but that song has been helpful, as it's very soothing."

"That song's specially designed for soothing and relaxation. It really seems to resonate with an exhausted generation of young people, doesn't it?"

Seeker is an ordinary person who makes videos of herself singing and posts them on the internet.

She had eighty thousand subscribers on WayTube, a video-hosting platform. Her channel was still small if you take into account that the criteria for a big channel was to have something between one hundred thousand and a million subscribers, and that was for both traditional celebrities and noncelebrities alike. But the original songs and cover videos that Seeker posted were high quality, and she got a pretty impressive number of views and "GOOD" ratings on each upload.

A cult favorite. Niche fame. Underground popularity. She'd be introduced with phrases like that if she was ever featured in mainstream media. An up-and-coming female singer. That's Seeker.

"Well, I'm glad you enjoyed it. Heh-heh-heh."

My voice was tinged with joy.

Well, why wouldn't it be? There's no need to hide it. I was the one who recommended Seeker to him, after all. It always felt great to hear someone say nice things about the stuff I liked.

"I was a bit doubtful when you sang the praises of her channel, but I must admit I have become quite addicted."

"It's reasonable to have reservations when you hear the words *unknown singer*, I guess."

"Ha-ha-ha. But one should try new things, is that not so? As reserved a gentleman as I may be… Oh, but there was one thing I thought was quite a shame."

"Oh, what might that be?"

Darn it, his quirk of using an old-fashioned way of speaking was rubbing off on me. Talking with Zeke was fun, but his way of speaking was infectious and a little annoying.

"She does not show her face in her videos."

"Well... It's a V channel."

V...meaning virtual. People who hide their true faces on WayTube, and instead use avatars that look like anime characters, are known as Vtubers, abbreviated as V.

Within the V sphere, there are further subcategories, like video creators and live streamers. Similar to Seeker, creators who mostly upload singing videos are sometimes called Vsingers, or virtual singers.

"But this means that she is, no doubt...a dog."

"I'll beat your a**!"

Unconsciously, an inappropriate expression escaped my mouth.

It was my policy to remain polite to anyone I chatted with online, no matter how close we might have been, but if someone tried to start trouble with me, then all bets were off. Like a proud country that refuses to negotiate with terrorists, I will mercilessly retaliate if anyone lobs verbal bombs at me.

"But she hides her true face because she lacks confidence, no? The only explanation can be that she is ugly, yes?"

"Some people value their privacy."

As I spoke, I swiftly unfollowed him on Twoitter.

"I heard it was better to have a little meat on the bones to produce a cute singing voice. She might be a bit fat, then?"

"Please recant that statement; it is extremely rude. Also, there are plenty of people out there who have cute voices and cute faces to match."

As I spoke, I unfriended him on *EPEX*.

"Well, Seeker's real face was leaked on the net, and it was, without a doubt, the face of a real dog."

"Ah, no, that was a fake."

"Is that so? What makes you so confident about that?"

"Er... Well... Um..."

My cursor paused on the screen, hovering above the UNFRIEND button on Wizcode.

Looking for a suitable excuse, I cast my gaze downward.

The time displayed on the bottom right corner of my screen read NINE PM.

"Oops, look at the time. I have to go and make dinner."

"Dodging the issue, eh?"

"No, no, you've got it all wrong. I'm the type who prefers to cook my own meals at home."

"Hmm, hmm. I can't see how I'll get any sleep tonight, after you've displayed such highly suspicious behavior…"

"Just put 'Laughter at the Bottom of the Ocean' on endless repeat; that'll sort ya. Okay, bye!"

I forcefully ended the conversation and quit the chat. Zeke seemed like he still had stuff he wanted to say, but if I had let him continue, I had the feeling I'd end up saying something I shouldn't.

But of course, I felt bad, so I re-followed him on Twoitter and friended him again on *EPEX*. Now we were even.

All right, I seemed to have gotten out of that one. I took a deep breath, turned off my computer, and stood up.

Leaving my room, I headed to the kitchen. Opening the cupboard above the sink, I grabbed a container of instant ramen from the precarious stack, ripped off the plastic with a practiced hand, and poured in boiling water from the electric kettle. Bon appétit.

What was that I said about preferring to cook for myself? Indeed, I do. I mean, it's far better than eating junk food or convenience store food for breakfast, lunch, and dinner. It's healthier. People who don't cook for themselves are total idiots, if you want my opinion. Yet…

(Such a hassle! I don't wanna!)

Yes, I prefer to cook for myself, but that's not to say that I actually DO it. People don't always do the things they believe to be best, after all.

Besides, even if you do want to cook, ingredients alone are quite expensive these days. A healthy diet is a luxury. Such is the world we live in now.

After preparing instant ramen for two, I grabbed two pairs of cheap blue-and-pink plastic chopsticks and hurriedly headed for the room next to mine.

"Time to eat."

I called out, then opened the door. Now, some might say it's not right to open the door before receiving a response, but those people don't know us. For us, this was a totally standard operating procedure.

The room was pitch-black inside. Even though I had just entered, there was no movement from anyone within.

I flipped on the lights to reveal the room in a terrible state. Clothes lying all over the place, mail-order cardboard boxes just discarded after being opened. It looked as if the room had been raided by burglars. But I did not panic at the sight.

After all, this was par for the course. This was the way this room was supposed to be. Honestly, if I had walked in to find it neat and tidy, then I'd start to worry that some sort of incident had occurred.

"You couldn't hear me again, could you? Far too absorbed, I keep telling you."

In the seemingly uninhabited room, I sighed and made my way to the closet with a practiced step.

"...Whoa!"

The very moment I opened the closet, a fog of muggy air came wafting out, and I reeled backward.

"I have no idea how you can stand being cooped up in there for such long periods of time."

"Mmm... What do you want, Gak?"

A sleepy voice, only perceptible if one strained their ears.

The creature that slowly turned around, emanating an aura of weakness akin to a dried-out jellyfish, with no signs of vitality at all, was a young girl.

Without a visit to the beauty salon in well over a year, her hair was left to grow long. It was an odd silver shade... But no, that was just my eyes playing tricks on me. Still, it seemed to have undergone some sort of chemical change. It hadn't been exposed to sunlight in a while and was only washed once every three days. In the dim darkness of the closet, it seemed to sparkle in an eerie way.

She wore a loose, baggy T-shirt that came down to her thighs. She clearly had no pants on. No doubt she only had underwear on underneath.

The only thing truly beautiful about her was her face. From my subjective point of view, I felt qualified to make that assessment. But her bangs were so long that they obscured her eyes and nose, making her features difficult to discern. If someone who didn't know about her pretty face saw her, they'd just assume she was ugly, and you could hardly blame them.

"Dinner, Shiika."

"…Pork bone broth?"

"One of them is. The other's chili tomato flavor. You can have whichever one you prefer."

"I don't like spicy food."

As she spoke, my little sister, Shiika Ikebukuro, snatched the container of pork bone broth noodles from my hand.

She peeled off the weakened sticker that held the lid down and frowned for a moment when the hot steam hit her face, then…

"Time to eat… Mm, that's good."

"It hasn't been three minutes yet."

"I like my noodles firm."

"It's instant ramen; they all turn out the same."

Sighing, I peered into the closet.

A closed-off space, devoid of air-conditioning.

This space, built specifically to store clothes, was obviously not being used for its intended purposes.

A desk and a PC. A condenser microphone, an audio interface, headphones, and sound-absorbing material to prevent reverb.

The desktop's wallpaper was an illustration of a beautiful female character with a steel harness on her head.

"Were you recording?"

"No. I've been editing."

"I see."

"Yeah."

"My friend raved about the last video."

"'Laughter at the Bottom of the Ocean'?"

"Yeah, that one."

"I see. So he likes blue. Poor guy."

"Poor guy?"

"Blue is the color people want to listen to when they're tired. He must be exhausted, I think, to like the song so much."

"Come to think of it, he did say he had insomnia."

...Of course, even after hearing that someone had raved about her singing, she didn't put on the slightest show of happiness. If it were me, I'd dance about and smirk and hum, and generally be in a great mood, but geniuses... They have sensibilities that are far beyond the comprehension of ordinary people like me.

If she wasn't my own sister, I would have no doubt spent my life having never come into contact with an overwhelming talent like hers.

That's right, Seeker, the genius Vsinger—the true identity of the mysterious girl who is secretly attracting attention in the underground scene—is none other than my own sister, Shiika Ikebukuro.

Just so we're clear here: I'm not the main character of this story.

I'm more like the storyteller, just an ordinary person who follows along after the talented genius named Shiika Ikebukuro.

In the process, I myself may get involved in some sort of side story. I might even get a girlfriend or climb the ladder of success, but those would be mere by-products. They'd have nothing to do with the main plot at all.

This is the story of Shiika Ikebukuro, who gains prominence as a singer and eventually influences people all over the world.

It is about talented young geniuses, and the struggles they face, and it all begins in a classroom where it turns out that looks are all you need.

oks Are All You Need

Chapter 0.5:
An Invitation

"I'm tired… I don't want to go outside… I'm gonna melt underneath the sunlight…"

"Please stop complaining."

Today the average temperature was slightly higher than one would have expected. It was still early April, before the yearly uniform change, and rather hot for spring break. Just walking around outside was enough to have beads of sweat form on your forehead that slid down your cheeks and dripped off your chin.

"I'll go for a walk two days next week instead of one—and make up for it then… Okay?"

"Nope."

"…You're so stingy, Gak. Stingy!"

"Ha-ha-ha. Your vocabulary is so limited that you lack the power to wound me. If you really want to make me mad, perhaps crack open a dictionary sometime."

"Unpopular kid. Virgin."

"Hey, there's a line you just shouldn't cross, you know???"

It was the middle of the week. There was nothing in particular going on, so why were Shiika and her elder brother out walking around on a boiling hot day like this one, you may ask? Well, unavoidable circumstances.

"We made a deal, didn't we? At least once a week, we'd go out for a walk for at least an hour. Now, I'll listen to you complain as much as you want, but this is one thing I won't budge on, okay?"

"Bleh."

My little sister is adorable, even when she pouts.

I'd love to respond to each one of her selfish complaints, I truly would, but I had to harden my heart sometimes, for the sake of her health.

Regular exercise is a vital, vital habit.

Especially for someone who's been a shut-in since junior high and rarely ever leaves the house. If I lost my sister to a lifestyle-related disease caused by lack of exercise, I wouldn't be able to live with myself.

We lived together, brother and sister, in a nondescript house in the suburbs, half an hour train ride from the city.

A short walk takes us to a rarely utilized public park. There's barely any playground equipment to speak of, which might be because of neighborhood noise complaints or simply a sign of the times. It would have been better overall if everything had been removed, but a shabby slide for kindergartners remained, located right in the middle of the park.

"Not a single kid to be seen, even though it's spring break."

"Well, yeah. It's more fun to play indoors now."

"A smartphone's all you need for entertainment, hmm? Kids these days don't know they're blessed. They get to grow up with all the online games a kid could want—and all the streaming material they could ever hope to watch. They should at least use our tax money to make a place for poor kids to play."

"I think this is far enough for me. Ahhh."

Shiika walked past me as I ranted and sat down on the slide.

"We're here for exercise. Don't sit down…"

"Sorry, no space for you, Gak."

"Oh, very mature."

Shiika, who was puffing out her cheeks and claiming sovereignty over the slide, didn't look like someone who'd just graduated from junior high school.

Her speech and behavior were childish, as if time stopped when she was still in elementary school, her development evidently delayed.

I'm certain there aren't many people who can tell that Shiika is a talented singer just by looking at her.

"By the way, Gak. Can I needle you a little?"

"Needle away. What's the issue?"

"If you care so much about health, then why are we always eating instant ramen?"

"Because we're broke."

"It said online that it's cheaper to cook for yourself."

"That information is outdated. Also, it's armchair theory. It's an opinion held by stupid people who haven't properly evaluated self-catering against other options."

"Really?"

"Would you like to go to the supermarket and check? Vegetables are expensive in this day and age."

"That's shocking."

"Your shock doesn't change the facts. Also, you don't look shocked at all."

Shiika spoke about our dining habits as if she were commenting on the personal affairs of a stranger.

In fact, Shiika doesn't know what our family's finances are like or what the circumstances are for our meals, and she doesn't really care. She just eats whatever's put in front of her. For better or worse, she has little interest in anything other than singing.

"We're not bringing in enough money?"

"Thanks to you, our income isn't bad... But to be honest, it's not enough to live on."

"That's shocking."

"Half of the advertising revenue from your I Tried Singing videos on WayTube goes to the rights holders of the original songs. The singer only gets a fraction of the revenue brought in from the views. And mass-producing original songs is not that easy."

"Oh."

"Can you try to sound more interested?!"

"It's too complicated. I don't get any of it. I'll just leave all that stuff up to you, Gak."

"Well, yes, that was what we agreed on from the start."

Shiika's lack of understanding about our financial situation was nothing new. In fact, it had been a constant thing since she started her activities as Seeker.

I was the one who noticed my sister's vocal talent and pushed her to use it. Now, this may be common among true prodigies, but Shiika has an almost fatal lack of desire to become famous or earn money with her talents. She just does whatever she wants. I take care of all the complex stuff that's unrelated to singing, like her virtual avatar—and managing money and rights. That was the arrangement we came up with when we started working together.

But now I'm in a fix. I've been doing what I can to make ends meet, but it's become impossible to get by on WayTube alone. And I know how unhealthy it is to continue eating instant ramen.

Three housewives with children in tow entered the park. This was clearly a great place to gossip while the kids ran around.

But when they saw us, they frowned and began whispering.

I could see the contempt in their eyes.

A man in dirty clothes, roaming around during the day like this... That's the way they were looking at me.

I'm not mistaken. I don't have a persecution complex.

I always get these kinds of looks when I go out shopping for dinner.

In this country, people act cold to the unemployed, who roam around freely during weekdays.

"Hmm, but still... If you wanna eat, you have to work."

I'm Gakuto Ikebukuro, eighteen years old.

I just wanted to live a life doing household chores, playing online games, and taking care of my incredibly talented sister, but perhaps it was time to face reality and pay my dues?

"I don't wanna..."

Just the thought of working in a company somewhere, the kind of place that wore you down with endless human interaction… It made me feel sick.

I wanted to find a way to live without working, somehow.

"""""Eek!!!"""""

The sound of women screaming rang out across the park, yanking me back to reality.

A pervert, perhaps? In broad daylight, though?

I looked over to where the screams had come from and saw that the housewives who'd been whispering before were now acting very strangely.

Holding up their phones in one hand, jumping up and down, waving their free hands. It was an undignified display, not how grown adults ought to behave at all.

But apparently those screams weren't screams of fear but of excitement.

"It's Kei!" "It's Kei, in the flesh!" "Oh lord, I can't believe it! I could die happy now!"

Their eyes had now taken on a different expression compared to when they'd been scowling at us two siblings moments before.

I noticed a black luxury car had parked near the entrance to the playground. The group of housewives had flocked over to the person who had just emerged from the car.

"Ah, excuse me. I'm in the middle of some work at the moment, so please save your adoration for later, ladies. ☆"

"""""Of course! ♪"""""

The man's voice was low and deep but had a lighthearted cadence.

The wall of housewives parted as they trilled a response that was as sweet as melted ice cream.

A lone middle-aged man appeared where they parted.

He must have been in his midthirties. He was relatively tall and wore an age-appropriate outfit, a suit in a subdued color.

He was handsome…maybe. To be honest, I couldn't really tell.

I mean, he was wearing black sunglasses and a cowboy hat, and I couldn't really see his face.

If not for the scruffy stubble on his exposed chin, I might have pegged him as a little younger.

The man walked straight over to Shiika and me.

"Hello there."

He greeted us, smiling.

"...Hi."

"..."

Exercising maximum vigilance, I looked up at him.

Shiika was silent. She held on to my sleeve shyly.

The suspicious gazes of the housewives were trained this way.

A junior-high-age kid and a high-school-age kid, being addressed all of a sudden by a suspicious man in glasses... I mean, it's exactly what it looked like... But the housewives seemed more skeptical of Shiika and me than they did of the guy.

...Who was he, some kind of celebrity?

"What business do you have with us?"

"Oh my. You know, it's been a long time since I've encountered someone who actually has their guard up around me. Don't you watch TV?"

"We don't even have a TV at home."

"Wow, the times, they are a-changin', huh? I guess kids these days are like that, spending all their time on WayTube... Right, Seeker? ☆"

"What...?!"

I stepped forward quickly, blocking Shiika from view.

They discovered her identity... But how? There was zero personal information in her channel's bio, and there shouldn't have been any possible way for anyone to track her down in person.

"Who the heck are you?"

"Eh-heh-heh. ♪ Ah, to think, the day has finally come where I actually have a use for these business cards."

With a creepy smile, the old man offered me his card.

* * *

Kei Tennouzu
President, Tennouzu Entertainment Co., Ltd.
Representative Director, Impachi Live Co., Ltd.
Special Scout, Ryouran Private High School

"Whoa…!"

The business card was a laundry list of impressive titles. It seemed too incredible to be real, but if it WAS real, then this guy who'd just appeared before us was surely on par with the fairy godmother who'd come to give Cinderella the pumpkin carriage.

My impression of the man changed, as the old…I mean, Kei Tennouzu, ah, heck, let's go with just Kei…as he gave a charming smile.

"The name's Kei Tennouzu. Former idol of Ignition, now a hot young businessman. Have you heard of Impachi Live?"

"No idea," Shiika responded.

"Huh?"

"I mean… Oh, oh, oh! My sister, that's just how she is! Sorry, I wasn't thinking! I'm her brother, her manager, see?!"

I pushed my sister, who was incapable of reading facial expressions, forward.

I was an expert at kissing up to people. I wasn't particularly smart, had no education, athletic ability, nor a special talent, nothing, really. But one thing I did have was the ability to wag my tail like a frenzied dog when I got a whiff of the opportunity to live without having to work. Oh, my pride? Dude, that thing was in tatters. Like an apple that'd been gnawed away by rats.

"Well, whatever. Let's get down to business, shall we?"

"Yes, yes, let's do that."

"I'm here for Shiika Ikebukuro. How would you like to turn her into a real entertainer?"

"Let's do it."

Zero hesitation on my part.

Kei Tennouzu…I mean, Kei…his eyes widened.

"Ah, but don't you want to think it over first? This is a huge turning point in both of your lives, you understand?"

"What's there to deliberate? You want to have Seeker make her major-label debut, right?"

"Well, eventually, that is the goal, yes…"

"CD sales, subscriptions, karaoke royalties, live performances, TV performances, commercials, we'll do anything. I can even lick shoes if you like. Trading sexual favors for career advancement… Well, I won't have Shiika doing that, but I don't mind biting a pillow or two."

"Hey, hey, hey, hold your horses. You're not a great listener, are you?"

He hurried to interrupt me, and I took a quick glance behind me. Perhaps he was worried about ordinary folk overhearing? But luckily, the housewives watching from the entrance to the park didn't appear to be able to hear us. They just stood rapturous, eyes sparkling.

"Unfortunately, you seem to have a big misunderstanding here, sonny."

"Oh, right, trading sexual favors probably shouldn't be done by proxy. Well, if that's the case, let's call the whole thing off."

"No, not that. Can we perhaps move on from that subject altogether?"

"Oh, sure."

"First off, I'm scouting Shiika Ikebukuro herself, not Seeker."

"You mean, not as a Vsinger, but…as a real singer?"

"Right. And one more thing, this isn't an invite that comes with a guaranteed major-label debut. You've read my business card, right?"

"Special Scout, Ryouran Private High School."

"A performing arts school, where students in all kinds of different artistic disciplines…music, acting, dance, and fashion…congregate. A school created to produce first-class stars who will one day dominate the top of the entertainment world. I would very much like for Shiika to enter this school."

All of a sudden, the heat that had risen up inside me cooled.

But of course, there's no such thing as a free lunch. There's always a catch.

"So it has to be her, in person? In the flesh, so to speak?"

"Yes, absolutely."

"So you didn't come to scout her after seeing her popularity as a Vsinger?"

"No, I didn't."

Kei... Ah, screw it, Kei Tennouzu shook his head.

"It's that singing ability. I want raw vocal talent. She can carry on her virtual stuff as a hobby if she likes, but I have high hopes for her future as a flesh-and-blood pop star."

"Why are you so fixated on the nonvirtual aspect?"

"Because virtual stuff doesn't work in the wider world. Of course, it's possible to gain tremendous popularity using a virtual avatar. But there is a target audience that simply cannot be reached without flesh-and-blood performers as a draw."

It felt like all of Shiika's efforts up until now were being thrown to the side, and it pissed me off, but I forced myself to take a deep breath to calm down.

This guy was a professional, so he had to know what he was talking about. To be honest, there was a part of me that realized there was a limit to the numbers we could reach with Shiika's virtual persona.

"All right, I understand the situation. I think there's merit, too, in what you say."

"Great. So she'll come, then?"

"However..."

I understood the situation. But...

"Unfortunately, we must decline. Shiika does not show her face."

"Mm-hmm... Mm-hmm..."

I turned as I spoke, and Shiika, hidden behind my back, gave a series of small nods.

"You won't change your mind?"

"No."

I answered without hesitation. I was absolutely adamant.

He could keep at it until he was blue in the face, but my answer would not change. If Shiika was capable of showing her true face on the world stage, then she would never have become a shut-in school truant in the first place.

"Living expenses will be paid. As long as she keeps her grades up."

"Huh?"

"All kids scouted personally by me, i.e., the ones who don't have to go through the admission process, the so-called Scout Kids, are completely exempt from paying admission fees and tutoring fees. There are no initial costs. She can receive a stipend for living expenses. And once she graduates, she'll have a one-way ticket to a life of first-class stardom. I doubt you'll find such a good deal anywhere else."

"Oof..."

Darn it. My resolve was weakening fast.

"With the advent of WayTube, anyone can make a living from their art, but when it comes to the I Tried Singing video trend, well, rights are split in half, so those videos don't generate much advertising revenue. And wouldn't you both like to eat really good food, more than just once in a blue moon?"

"Guh..."

I clenched my jaw. My determination was like Jell-O.

"Slurrrp."

Shiika was drooling, too.

"Well, if you're not interested, I did my best. I'll have that business card back."

"...!"

"Huh?"

My fingers clamped down on the business card even as he tried to take it away.

Kei Tennouzu tugged, but it was wedged firmly between my fingers, as if glued there, and didn't give at all.

"Shiika. You don't want to show your face or go to school. Do you?"

"No. Don't wanna."

"But you want to eat delicious food, don't you?"

"Wanna eat."

"Could you handle it? Going to school, I mean?"

"I think I could just about manage. As long as you can be in the same class, Gak."

"...You heard her. Would such an arrangement be possible?"

I looked cajolingly at Kei Tennouzu again. He paused and seemed to consider something deeply, stroking his chin.

"All right, it's a deal!"

He showed me his white teeth and gave me a thumbs-up.

"Wow..."

"Food...!"

"We'll pay living expenses for two, as well."

"Are you some kind of angel?"

"An extra side dish...!"

Shiika and I clasped hands, our eyes sparkling.

To be honest, having to leave home was a big hassle, and I never wanted to find myself in a school environment again. But the stomach wants what it wants.

And it would be a million times better to slack off at a school than work.

Besides, if I could be in the same class as Shiika, that alone would make it completely different from the school life I'd experienced in the past. With that one condition, a lot of hurdles had been cleared.

Because as long as I'm around to keep an eye on her, I know Shiika won't come to any kind of harm.

So with that being the case...I guess I can handle going to school again.

Even though I thought there was pretty much zero chance of Shiika becoming an entertainer if she had to show her face.

Still, all we had to do was bide our time. Collect the living expenses for the next three years, while uploading videos as Seeker on the side. Then all we had to do was say "no thanks" to Shiika becoming an in-person entertainer. Reap only the benefits and bow out when the situation became inconvenient.

A perfect plan with no possible drawbacks! Ha-ha-ha!

"Then it's decided. Ah, these are the enrollment forms. Please submit them by the beginning of next week. Detailed materials will be sent later. As soon as spring break is over, you will join us at the entrance ceremony. With that in mind, please make whatever arrangements you need to be prepared."

"Right! Thanks very much!"

"Shiika Ikebukuro… I look forward to seeing how our academy evolves, with the entrance of such a prodigious vocalist."

Then Kei Tennouzu…ah, correction, Kei…gave us a stylish wave and walked off.

"Those kids were just scouted by Kei himself!" "They must be future megastars!" "Eek, how amazing! We should go and grab their autographs while we've got the chance!"

The eyes of the housewives by the park's entrance were completely different now.

Thoughts of money swirled in my mind.

"…Still, I won't fleece them…too much. Heh. Heh-heh-heh."

A lower-middle-class kid like myself could get carried away.

"Hey, Gak?"

And then we have my sister, who's not just a normal lower-middle-class human, but an actual musical prodigy.

"What's performing arts?"

"You…listened to that whole conversation without knowing what that meant?"

"All I got from it was that you and I can go to school together and eat yummy food."

"There was quite a lot more to it than that…"

Shiika's vocal talents had been highly evaluated, and she had been granted entrance to a top performing arts school.

Those two things alone would be enough to have aspiring talents all over the country freaking out, but Shiika seemed almost…placid.

No doubt, my sister has a screw loose somewhere.

A school where the elite of the entertainment world congregated…

I was a little worried about how two shut-ins like us would fare in a place like that. But when I looked at Shiika, I felt all my doubts fade away.

I mean, what could possibly go wrong? My sister, after all, has got some serious talent.

Chapter 1:
Entering the Academy

A little under a half hour's walk from downtown, the neon signboards and the hustle and bustle of the people disappeared. The area had a pleasant vibe, with its uniform apartment blocks, spacious green parks, and all the shops and convenience stores you could need for an easy life.

But in the midst of it, one building stood out in an odd way.

Ryouran Private High School.

The main school building had retro-style redbrick walls. There was an outdoor stage for performances, an indoor pool and gym, a memorial hall preserving the achievements of alumni, and several studios for lessons, among other facilities. The buildings around us all had stylish architecture. Even though we were there for the entrance ceremony, it felt more like we were taking a sightseeing tour.

Seeing the uniformed students heading toward the auditorium reassured me that I had the correct time and location for the entrance ceremony.

Still, I couldn't deny that I felt completely out of place.

All around us were beautiful people.

Academic ability aside, the ratio of gorgeous faces would have to be something like 80 percent.

They all had the standard, cute idol good looks, the kind you see on

TV, and everyone had a slim build and good posture. In their tailored uniforms, they reached extraordinary heights of conventional attractiveness.

Then there was me. With bedhead, a hunched back, and bags under my eyes. My presence was dragging the beauty ratio way down.

No doubt Shiika and I were standing out in a bad way. Passing students, current ones and newbies alike, were all staring at us.

"Hey, is he a freshman as well?"

"No way. He couldn't have passed the entrance requirements with a drab face like that. No doubt he's just here to deliver something a sibling forgot."

"But he's wearing a uniform."

"What, seriously? Then I guess he really is a student? That girl he's with, though, her hair is a total bird's nest. And she clearly has no sense of style."

"Sometimes people slip through the net and manage to get in. No doubt they'll end up flunking out right away, though."

"Oh, you're totally right."

Shut up. You think I don't know all that? And hey! To me, Shiika is adorable! You just can't see it 'cause her bangs are covering her eyes! You have no idea what kind of effect she might have on the beauty ratio at this school! Although, I guess that was just my personal opinion.

"...Well, it's understandable. When you think about the kind of world these students are aiming for, then our dull appearances just come across as disrespectful."

The entertainment industry is notorious for being hard to break into.

The average number of applicants for auditions held by entertainment agencies exceeds thirty thousand, but only one in a thousand pass.

Although there are probably some opportunists who audition just for the fun of it, if you factor in the people who reckon they've got an actual shot at success, that's still a crazy number of applicants. Then if you think about the number of people who were half-assed about it and didn't end up making it to the audition, then it's pretty easy to guess how many people want to enter the entertainment world.

Shiika and I entered this school with the ulterior motive of getting some help with our living expenses.

Trying to stand out in a competitive environment like this would be playing a losing game. Even if I did have that kind of goal for myself, there's no way I'd make it through without being crushed.

But unlike me, a totally ordinary guy, Shiika has real talent. She might actually have a shot.

Shiika was currently humming beside me without a care in the world.

"La-di-da."

"You're in a good mood. Don't you find this atmosphere overwhelming?"

"Such a nice breeze out today. The sound of it rustling the leaves on the trees is just perfect today. Ah, it feels so good."

"Is it different from usual…?"

"It's usually transparent. But today it's greenish-yellow."

"Nope, no idea."

"This school is full of all kinds of colors."

I blinked, looking at Shiika's profile as she gazed around at the school. This was directly connected to the reason Shiika kept singing.

There were people working hard at their rehearsals on the outdoor stage, even though it was the morning of the entrance ceremony. No doubt there was some sort of music being played in the studio. I couldn't hear any of it, not through those soundproof walls, but Shiika… Whenever Shiika's ears picked up on even the slightest sound wave, she "saw" it as color.

No doubt Shiika was able to "see" all the sounds that were being created throughout this entire school.

"This might actually be fun."

"…Yeah. Let's hope."

Hearing Shiika's slightly cheerful tone, I found myself smiling.

Neither of us had pleasant memories of school, but if Shiika could manage to enjoy this, then I couldn't ask for anything more.

And so Shiika and I headed to the large auditorium where the entrance ceremony was to be held, our hearts filled with faint hope for our new life.

◊ ◊ ◊

The large auditorium lacked oxygen, making me feel drowsy. The place was poorly ventilated.

This might have been a fancy performing arts school, but it was still a regular high school entrance ceremony. It was no different than any other high school. Just pompous people lecturing us for what felt like an eternity of boredom.

The other students looked half asleep as well, which proved that my mindset toward it all wasn't just because I had mediocre sensibilities and a twisted personality.

The high, reedy-voiced rhetoric spewed by the school officials was so long and so tedious that the hard chairs, usually impossible to sleep in, started feeling as cozy as a baby's cradle.

Beside me, Shiika was asleep. Three minutes in, she'd nodded off.

She rested her small head on my shoulder and breathed lightly, totally at ease, just as if she was at home.

I was able to stay awake thanks to Shiika. If I fell asleep, there'd be nothing propping up her head, and she'd tumble off the chair, making a racket. If we made ourselves conspicuous, we might have our living expenses cut, which would suck, or in the worst-case scenario, we might get suspended or even expelled from the school.

I can't sleep. We need tomorrow's meal ticket. However, if this ceremony drags on any longer, I'm not sure I can control myself.

Please. Please let this end.

Perhaps the heavens heard my wish. Sudden noise disrupted the drowsy, soporific air of the auditorium.

It wasn't displeasing at all. In fact, it was an almost welcome sensation of uneasiness.

"…And now, to the congratulatory address. Here is our current student representative, Io Kanda, third-year student and top of the Talent Department."

"Thank you."

Summoned by the MC, a female student stood up and approached the stage.

She was like a beautiful flower in human form.

Every eye in the auditorium must have been on her.

Beauty is in the eye of the beholder, just like ugliness. There's no such thing as an absolute consensus on what beauty is. Yet even a warped individual like myself who tends to look at everything from unconventional angles had to admit that this girl was a stunner.

First off, her posture was perfect.

She stood with a straight back, and even when walking, she maintained balance.

Character and intelligence oozed from the confident way she held herself. It was obvious she was skilled at both academics and sports.

Second, her figure was beautiful.

Even when she wore the standard uniform, her curves were apparent—her waist was narrow and her abdomen toned.

Her curves were like art; they made you want to admire her just as if she were a Greek statue—not in a vulgar way or anything.

And of course, her face was beautiful.

Even in a school of good-looking girls and boys, her overwhelming beauty stood out.

"It's Io Kanda."

"Seriously? You mean THAT Io Kanda?"

"No way! I've seen her in a TV drama!"

"Yikes, she's got the aura of an actual professional. I'm breaking out in a cold sweat."

Noise erupted in the auditorium. All eyes were fixed on the girl onstage, and multiple whispered conversations about her took place.

Apparently, this person was someone special from the point of view of the other students as well.

I don't usually watch TV, so I'd have no way of knowing, but she appeared to be someone who was already famous and in the media. In other words, she was a bona fide resident of the entertainment world,

the world all these other students were aiming to join. No wonder this
girl seemed so different.

Io Kanda stood on the stage, adjusted the height of the microphone,
and cleared her throat. Then she took a big breath.

"Quit your grunting, pigs! You don't have the right to even speak
words!" she bellowed in an abominable voice.

...What the heck?

The auditorium fell silent. Everyone was shocked by what had just
come out of her mouth.

Even Shiika had woken up.

She took her head off my shoulder and gazed at Io Kanda onstage,
eyes wide.

"That voice just now...," Shiika muttered.

"She was really yelling, huh?"

"No, not that. That was a really wonderful voice."

"Say what?"

I wasn't following.

Staring at Io Kanda, Shiika's eyes shone like a curious cat.

"It was loud but crystal clear. The way the sound hits the mic, her
projection, it was all just perfect. Smooth."

"Oh yeah, now that you mention it. There was no distortion at all."

"And she got everyone in the auditorium to listen to her."

Shiika was right.

No one was chattering any longer. Io Kanda had been the center of
everyone's attention and was merely the subject of conversations. But
now she had taken the lead role in this scenario.

Her expression switched from angry to smiling in an instant.

"...Currently, I'm acting in a production where I play an individual
who makes remarks such as those."

She spoke with a mischievous, relaxed tone.

It was like a clear mountain stream, the polar opposite to her previous harsh bellowing.

After that, Kanda's congratulatory address was full of trite and bland clichés, too boring to even transcribe. Despite this, the new students listened quietly and solemnly until she was done.

Grabbing the audience right off the bat makes a big difference, I noted with surprise.

"Each one of you is a precious little flower bud, possessing both sweet nectar and poison. I hope that you all bloom beautifully, so that our generation can be known as the ones who really made Ryouran High blossom. I hope that you will all cherish your time spent growing and flourishing in this academy's hallowed classrooms. And that's all from me, Io Kanda, third-year top student here at Ryouran High."

Finishing with a flourish, she shuffled her notes and bowed.

Clap-clap-clap... The applause resounded like torrential rain.

Even I found myself applauding. But I think I was impressed in a different way compared to everyone else.

The content of her speech was generic, but the impact of her intro and the way her final words were perfectly original... It was all nicely handled in a way that I found admirable.

Cutting unnecessary corners is a type of craftsmanship that often goes unnoticed. For a guy like me, whose only wish is to slack off as much as possible, it seems like the kind of thing I should try to emulate.

Shiika clapped as well, but she did it in her usual way, *clappity-clappity*. A little odd, but it was her own way of showing appreciation.

"That was amazing. So that's what this school's top students are like."

"Yeah. I like her voice. It has a color I've never seen before."

"Really? What kind of color?"

"I don't know. The closest thing to it is purple."

Unusual. Shiika never usually has trouble articulating colors.

"But it's paler than normal purple, almost translucent. It sparkles."

"Maybe it's because Io Kanda is especially talented."

"I don't know. Maybe?"

"Well, in any case. You might encounter a lot of colors you've never seen before."

"Yeah. I can fill my palette with new sounds."

La-di-da, she hummed. Seeing her, I couldn't help but think... Yep, I'm glad we decided to come to this school, even if we only came for that stipend money.

◊ ◊ ◊

I take back what I said. We never should have come to a school like this one.

In the first year Music Department classroom, I sat with my cheek propped up in one hand, staring with glazed eyes at the other students who were all enjoying themselves.

Shiika and I sat in the far corner of the back row. This school seemed to have a free seating arrangement. No one had assigned desks, so students could sit wherever they wanted. Only the lockers installed along the hallway for students to store their stuff were assigned.

It was rare for high schools in Japan to allow students to sit wherever they liked. It was only common at colleges, but since this was a performing arts school, its rules seemed defined by a different set of values compared to ordinary high schools.

Still, this kind of setup was convenient for Shiika and me.

If the seating had been decided by a lottery system, or at the homeroom teacher's discretion, or some other irrational method, then I might have been separated from Shiika, and that would have been terrible.

I was certainly glad that Shiika wouldn't be all on her own in this kind of shitty environment.

Before my eyes, conversations straight out of hell were taking place—and had been taking place for a while now.

"Hey, did you hear? That jerk Sawamura is apparently in the Fashion Department."

"No way! That uggo?"

"Right? They don't have any fashion sense. It's too funny!"

"Ha-ha, maybe they're planning on having a high-school-ugly-duckling-to-swan type of transformation! But it's not like going from junior high to high school has any magical ability to fix that, now, is there? Points for trying, though!"

"You said it!"

…And that's the kind of stuff they were saying.

Sawamura was no doubt a student who got bullied in junior high. The vitriol it takes to continue ragging on someone even at this stage of one's educational career. Staggering.

Listening to this crap had put me in the worst mood. You could hardly blame me. This was a live demonstration of exactly the reason why I didn't want to come to school.

"But seriously, doesn't the competition seem subpar this year? Even the kids who had to pass the exam to get in don't seem to have that X factor."

"Right?"

The voices had grown quieter. No doubt, when you're openly dissing other individuals present in the classroom, you don't really want to blast it.

…But I mean…I can hear you, you know? And it's really obvious that you keep looking this way. You're not exactly doing a good job of hiding it, now, are you?

"No point trying to be the best this year, even for us, though, is there?"

"You're so right. It's totally impossible."

"No one's got a shot at the top spot with Erio around."

"I know, right?"

"You'll be aiming for top of the grade, won't you, Erio?"

The silly, flirty girls fixed their eyes on one of the other students. A girl with a striking appearance.

Pale skin like a white female wolf running through a snow-covered landscape. Refined features. Her long hair was dyed in a beautiful contrast of black and gray, and her accessories, large earrings and a choker around her neck, looked amazing on her.

"Oh stop, you're embarrassing me."

The girl, Erio—embodiment of style and coolness—narrowed her eyes at her twittering friends as she spoke.

"Competing with high school kids will only degrade me."

"Woo! You're amazing!"

"You're easily the best in the whole school, Erio!"

Erio spoke like a queen addressing her lowly subjects, who clustered around her, jabbering loudly.

Can't you keep it down? You're only talking that loud to garner attention. To be honest, I can't stand people like that.

"Hey, Erio, you're releasing a song from Queen Smile soon, right?"

The loud conversation was continuing.

"Making your major-label debut in freshman year of high school… That's just so Erio Shibuya!"

"Heh-heh. Well, it's all about talent. Talent and ability."

Erio Shibuya was boasting.

Keep that up and your nose will grow as long as a *tengu*.

"It hasn't released yet, so don't talk about it too much, okay? Also, make sure all of you go and buy the CD. We may be in the age of streaming, but CD sales still count for a lot, you know."

"We will!"

"Komae was the composer, right? Ah, the golden team, rushing to take the entertainment world by storm!"

"Yes, Nokia, right?"

Shibuya went out of her way to mention the first name of the boy they were discussing.

Her voice even went up an octave.

"There isn't much competition in his age group, but Nokia is still exceptional. The songs he writes really make my voice pop. He's the best partner."

"Woo! Yes, yes, you go so well together!"

"Oh, how I admire you both, the beautiful boy and girl genius duo!"

…How much longer will this conversation last?

While I was shooting an icy look at the excited group of girls, a lone male student approached them.

He was a tall, slender, handsome guy, with voluminous red hair softly tied up in an idol-ish hairstyle. His eyes were sharp but attractive, and his face was slim and regal. The literal walking embodiment of a beautiful youth. His natural features were already unquestionably wonderful, but the earring glinting in his ear showed that he had a great sense of style to top it all off.

He and I were wearing the same uniform, but that's pretty much where the similarities ended.

The flashy red-haired boy casually touched the shoulder of one of the girls who was raving about Shibuya.

"What's all the commotion? Could it be that you're bad-mouthing me?"

He spoke as if deeply hurt.

"K-Komae?!"

The female student shouted his name.

So this must have been the noteworthy composer who they were just discussing, Nokia Komae. The beautiful boy and girl genius duo... I see. With those looks, that evaluation makes sense.

With his hand on the girl's shoulder, Komae spoke again, bringing his lustrous lips, shiny and deeply colored as if he was wearing lipstick, closer to her ear.

"Now, now. If you go bad-mouthing me, the other girls won't give me the time of day any longer."

"W-we would never bad-mouth you... Your hand... It's on my shoulder..."

"Right. You're down for what this indicates, yes?"

"Wh-what does it indicate?"

"Can I fall for you? Can I make you mine? If so, I'll forgive you for all of it."

"Wh-whaaat?!!!"

"Nokia. Your jokes are in bad taste. Can you please stop hitting on my friends?"

"Oh, don't be so scary. Scowling like that will ruin your adorable face, Erio."

"Gosh, you're annoying. Go away."

"All right, all right, this jerk is leaving now. Ah, but you're always welcome to ask me out on a date. I'll be waiting for your call. ☆"

Winking, Komae walked off, and the girls erupted into shrieks.

Even Shibuya, who was snarky with him, seemed tickled by his compliments about her looks. Though her brow was raised, her cheeks were tinted pink.

Seeing such a spectacle, as a normal freshman, there was only one feeling that arose in my chest.

…Gag me.

"…Gag me."

"Huh?"

For a moment, I was taken aback and had to wonder if I might have said that aloud without realizing it. But no, it was a female voice, and it came from the neighboring desk.

Not from where Shiika sat.

Shiika was fast asleep on her desk. I could see the drool dripping onto her folded arms underneath and spreading across the surface of the desk. Even though she's my little sister, I have to say that it takes some cheek to fall asleep at the start of homeroom on the first day of a new school.

So anyway, the person who'd just spoken my thoughts aloud wasn't my sister, but someone else entirely. Apparently, the voice I'd heard belonged to the girl sitting on my other side, and she turned her head when she noticed my surprised reaction.

Looking at her face from the front, I felt utter and total relief.

In this school full of beautiful boys and girls, the female student in front of me had a surprisingly ordinary, plain appearance.

Now, you couldn't go calling a girl like this ugly, but at the same time, she didn't fit into the "beautiful" category.

She had natural black hair, the color her parents' genes had gifted her. She wore it in a smooth, short, straight bob that seemed to have been styled with nothing stronger than plain water. Her figure… Well, she wasn't fat, but a career in modeling was out of the question.

Her looks were average, and she was reassuringly ordinary. And she was staring at me with a suspicious look in her eyes.

"You're thinking something rude, aren't you? I can tell by your expression."

"No, no, no. We haven't met before, have we?"

"Were you listening to me just now? Don't tell anyone what I said."

"I won't."

I hate gossip and those who tattle the most.

Also…

"I kinda felt the same way as you."

"Oh, you're an ally? Well, why didn't you say so?"

The female student smiled, looking pleased.

Her tone and facial expressions were somewhat boyish. For a moment, I thought I might die from the tension, since I honestly didn't have much experience talking to real girls, but she seemed like the type I'd actually be fine around. In that sense, she had a comforting presence.

"I'm Mana Akihabara. Akihabara's a mouthful, so call me Akiba or Mana, whichever you prefer."

"Then I'll call you Akiba."

It was easier to talk to a tomboy, sure. But calling her so casually by her first name… That was too high of a hurdle for me.

"What's your name? I don't know your face. You must have gone through the application process, right?"

"I'm Gakuto Ikebukuro. That's my sister, Shiika, asleep over there."

"Sister? So you're twins?"

"No, no, special circumstances. Actually, I'm eighteen, two years older than her."

"Wow, you're practically middle-aged."

"Don't call me middle-aged. Like I said, there are special circumstances."

To reassure her, I added that Shiika was sixteen, the same age as her.

Akiba put her finger to her chin, looking thoughtful.

"Eighteen… So you had to repeat at least two grades before finally entering Ryouran? Wow, you're tenacious."

"No, not at all. I just came here because of the scout."

"Oh, I see, so you were one of the kids who got scouted... Wait, you got SCOUTED?!"

I was shocked by her sudden booming voice.

...Hey, did you hear that? This guy got scouted.

...Are you serious? I mean, okay, I don't remember seeing him in junior high, but seriously? That dork got scouted?

All eyes in the classroom were on us, and they were bright with curiosity.

Even the influential kids like Erio Shibuya and Nokia Komae, who'd been giving off a glowing aura at the center of class up until this moment, were now looking our way.

Huh? Things got intense all of a sudden.

"Being scouted is, like, SUPER rare! Gakuto, who exactly are you?"

"Ah, no, well, to be precise, it wasn't actually me; it was my sister, you see?"

"Has she been active as a singer?! Does she do I Tried Singing videos?! Vocaloid?! An indie idol?!"

"Can you please chill out?!"

Pressed back against my chair, I tried to come up with some quick answers. It's kind of a thing for Vsingers to go to great lengths to conceal their true identity behind their anime avatar, so I had to be smart here. I had to make sure I didn't say the wrong thing.

Panicking, I finally came up with something.

"...She... She won a local karaoke tournament. She's kind of, uh, locally famous?"

"Oh..."

They seemed convinced. Maybe.

"Hmm, well, there are scouts everywhere, even at karaoke tournaments, I guess... And some people get scouted if they're knockout beauties... Oh, it seems she's waking up."

"Mnyah... Nyam nyam."

No doubt due to all the noise in the classroom, Shiika finally stirred, shoulders twitching, and she slowly lifted her head.

All eyes focused on Shiika, trying to appraise the face of this girl who had apparently been scouted.

Shiika, unaware that she'd become the center of attention, sat up with an open, innocent expression and let out a huge yawn.

"Mmn... Gak, good morning..."

"Uh, yeah. Morning. Your hair... It's all over the place."

"Hmm?"

Shiika tilted her head and tried to flatten down her bed hair. But as soon as she moved her hands away, it sprang back.

It felt almost like a balloon of expectation that had been inflating in the classroom had suddenly deflated.

When they heard she was scouted, they all wondered what kind of person she was, but she seemed to be a simple country girl who was just good at singing in her hometown. It looked like there were disappointing scouting results here on a yearly basis.

I could hardly blame them for thinking this. I mean...

Shiika, looking up, was a mess. Her hair had grown out, and it was obvious that she hadn't gone to a beauty salon in a long time. Her cheeks and eyelids were swollen from sleeping on her folded arms, and her eyes were red and bleary. She even had drool marks on her chin.

All the signs of dishevelment that one could think of, on full display. Ah, but still, I totally think she's well within the parameters of what you could call cute. But in a classroom like this, where kids with a high aesthetic sense gather, her cuteness would probably fly under the radar.

All right, nothing to see here. That's how they reacted. The students, having lost interest, let their gazes wander elsewhere.

I didn't feel sorry about it. I never wanted us to draw attention, so actually, I preferred it this way.

"Gakuto. And Shiika."

Akiba tapped me on the shoulder.

"We're allies. Let's be friends, all right?"

She gave us a double thumbs-up, and just like that, she'd decided we were all buddies.

…Allies in what? Being dorks? Well, it was the truth at least. So no harm, no foul.

◊ ◊ ◊

"Yawwwn!!! I am SO tired!"

"Me too, Gak…"

It was around two PM. After leaving school, we boarded the train, and when we got off at our local station, I heaved a huge sigh. I was exhausted.

Even though the school day was short, just the entrance ceremony and a very short homeroom—all of which was done by the afternoon—I still felt a sense of overwhelming fatigue, as if I was being tethered down by shackles.

Attending school, commuting by train, and talking to other people for the first time in a while… There was so much I wasn't used to. If someone suffering from a lack of exercise suddenly sprints at full speed, they'll get horrible muscle soreness. I had the mental version of that. Honestly, I was dead on my feet.

Having to introduce myself was one of the hardest things. I wish these things didn't have a turn-based system. The way everyone's eyes fall on you when it's your turn… I can never get used to it. It always sucks. I was a gloomy type of person who just wanted to live life behind the scenes, so when the spotlight fell on me like that, I wanted to die.

I think I managed to introduce myself, but I have no idea how I came off to the others. Um, I, uh, ahem, well, but… I hope I didn't sound like that. I bet I did, though. Ugh, I could die.

Standing at the crosswalk waiting for the light, I was consumed by these kinds of thoughts. I felt like leaping out into the road. I was glad Shiika was with me. No way would I go jumping in front of traffic with her around.

"You know, Shiika, you did a pretty good job of introducing yourself."

"I practiced. Had it down pat. My Vsinger routine."

"Seriously? 'I'm Shiika Ikebukuro. Nice to meet you. No questions.' You practiced that? Amazing."

"And my bangs helped. It was nice not being able to really see anyone."

"Oh yeah."

As the day passed, Shiika's bedhead and overgrown bangs had calmed down.

It seemed a shame to hide her cute face, but to her, it was a kind of interpersonal defense mechanism.

Shiika sees sounds as colors.

The colors she sees are a visualization of the emotions and various kinds of energy contained in specific sounds, with sounds produced by bad feelings having an unbelievably ugly, almost stagnant color.

In junior high school, Shiika withdrew from class, unable to stand all the colors, and became a shut-in.

Overgrown bangs helped to block her vision, making the world a little less visible to her.

It could be inconvenient. But for Shiika, it was easier to live like this.

The light turned green. I looked left and right. After confirming the cars had safely stopped, I took Shiika's hand, and we hurried across the road.

Inattentive Shiika has a bad habit of stopping at random moments and staring into space, so I have to keep constant watch over her. To be honest, it's more like I'm her nurse. She can't really do anything except make music.

When we reached the sidewalk on the other side, I felt relieved. Walking down a deserted path, we were just about to pass the neighborhood park when I spotted a boy, maybe a local junior high school student, filming something with his phone. That suddenly reminded me of something.

"By the way, about the thing the homeroom teacher mentioned… Are you going to do it?"

"Do…it?"

"You know. It's one of the Ryouran High rules. Every student has to set up an Impachi Live account."

"Impachi Live… Oh, right."

"You have a vague recollection of it? Come on, Shiika. Our food budget depends on your grades."

"I don't really wanna..."

"I know how you feel! I know! But please! For the sake of our food supply!"

I got down on my knees and pressed my forehead to the asphalt. The ground, warmed by the spring sunshine, felt hot against my head. I was glad it wasn't summer. Although I'd never get down on the ground and grovel outside in the summer in the first place.

After that scene in the classroom, where the school hierarchy was put on full display, and after the hellish round of self-introductions was over, our female homeroom teacher explained the rules of Ryouran High. They were unthinkable, completely unorthodox, nothing like normal high school rules.

Ryouran Private High School Student Rules

1. **All current students must create and operate an Impachi Live account.**

   Even if you have a private account, create a new account and start from scratch.

2. **Post videos and streams using the account created in Rule #1.**

   The content you upload and the frequency of your uploads is up to your discretion, but please refrain from violating any public orders or morals.

   You are free to create whatever content you desire, but if you break the rules, you will be banned just like a normal user, so be careful about what you post.

3. **The monthly living allowance will be determined by our evaluation of your account.**

   The evaluation will take into account the number of

views, Likes, and the amount of donations, etcetera, acquired each month.

The algorithm that determines the rating is private, and we will not respond to any inquiries regarding this.

4. Follow the rules and have fun expressing yourself!

"That old fart Tennouzu hid something important from us. He did say we'd be paid living expenses based on performance, but he didn't mention that it was tied to online success. This is meant to be a performing arts school! How can they predict online success? It's unbelievable!"

Since Shiika's and my grades would be combined, it didn't really concern us, but surely, normal students would find such a system frustrating.

Or perhaps the students who aim to be first-class entertainers will be able to flourish in this sort of system?

Either way, it struck me as pretty cutthroat.

Shiika tilted her head, reading the list of school rules that I'd just pulled up on my phone.

"Uploads? Streams? Like on WayTube?"

"Something like that. But rather than nerdy geeks, the people who watch Impachi Live tend to be younger, with more female viewers in the mix. And it's a given that those on Impachi Live will show their faces."

"Show their faces... So Seeker wouldn't work?"

"Nope."

"...There has to be some other way, Gak?"

"There isn't."

I did not have the authority to change the rules. I mean, if I had that kind of power, I wouldn't need to be attending school.

"You can't use your Seeker persona at all."

"What?"

"You're attending school as Shiika Ikebukuro, right? The other students are going to see your account and know it's you. The little slice of freedom you carved out on the web is of no use to us now."

"I don't like that."

"Right? I know you don't like showing your face, but we have to eat. I'll take care of everything else, but you need to do this one part. Please!"

"...Grudgingly."

"Are you doing this or not?"

"Sushi."

"What?"

"I want to eat sushi. The good stuff, not conveyor-belt sushi. If I can have that, then I'll do it."

"Guh... I don't remember teaching you such mature negotiation tactics?! Who the heck taught you that?! I'm gonna curse them! May they never get a girlfriend! That'll teach them to go teaching my little sister weird stuff!"

"I was just copying what you do, Gak."

"Ack! Okay, I take it back! Cancel the hex!"

Was I the root of the evil after all...?

My shoulders slumped in disappointment. I glanced at Shiika. Her pure, innocent eyes were shining with anticipation.

"I can't wait. Sushi. Yayyy."

"...! All right! Let's go! Sushi!"

"Yeaaah!"

I've never been able to resist Shiika's pleading.

Still, things would probably be fine. With Shiika's vocal abilities, we should be able to get the minimum number of views we need even without having to rely on Seeker. Our living costs were all but assured, so what was the harm on splurging on sushi, the revolving kind or the non-revolving kind?

◊ ◊ ◊

After eating a ton of sushi that was ridiculously expensive, we arrived home, and I shook Shiika awake from her post-meal nap to have her prepare for streaming.

Eating to her heart's content, then falling asleep completely satisfied... Such devilish behavior.

If you don't work, you don't get to eat. Or to put it another way, if she didn't earn money through streaming online, I'd never be able to recoup the funds I'd just blown on all that sushi.

"Um... I think this is the correct setup. Just got to peel this poster off the wall; don't want anyone seeing this Seeker illustration..."

The closet of Shiika's room was her secret recording space. Stepping on discarded underwear and candy wrappers, I fiddled with the PC settings, set up her streaming mic, and adjusted the orientation of the phone stand.

All the videos Seeker had uploaded until now were I Tried Singing videos, and so the correct setup wasn't in place.

But her brother, who anticipated this situation, has all the equipment needed to get her stream-ready!

I dream of the day when Shiika can get over her dislike of speaking. Then she can earn big money as a live streaming Vsinger who does Super Chats.

I'm Gakuto Ikebukuro, and I'll spare no effort when it comes to earning enough money to live without having a job.

In any case, just by doing a little tweaking like this, I can create the perfect streaming environment.

"All right, here's all the essentials you need for streaming."

"Oh. *Clap-clap.*"

"Now, you know what you need to do for your first stream, right?"

"Show big boobs and dance."

"Technically correct but fatally wrong at the same time."

Certainly, there are some broadcasters who use such physical traits to lure male viewers and pull in the numbers.

But that comes with the risk of being banned, and more importantly, it's not the kind of content that Shiika should be making.

"First, a simple self-introduction stream. I did some research on my phone while we were eating sushi, and it seems there are some active

Impachi Live viewers who are really excited about the streaming debuts of Ryouran High's new students. Some of these viewers will actually check the #RyouranNewFaces hashtag looking for self-intro streams, and they'll go back and watch all the archives. If you can grab their attention, we'll be able to get a stable number of views. Apparently, each year there are a handful of students who go viral and easily shoot up the ladder to stardom."

"Huh. Convenient."

"I'm just glad we're fortunate enough to be able to use a hashtag that's guaranteed to be seen by viewers."

It took a while for Seeker to gain a fan base on WayTube.

It was a harsh world, a veritable red ocean, as the number of virtual idol-like accounts kept increasing by the dozen each month. The kind of place where looking good in the real world was no longer enough to garner attention.

...This could be our big chance.

It was Shiika's vocal ability that helped establish a fan base on Way-Tube in the first place, a site where it's hard to gain a foothold.

On a platform with a guaranteed chance of catching people's attention, Shiika would be a hot topic from day one, and from there, our numbers would grow exponentially.

"Heh-heh... Mwah-ha-ha... We've already won!"

"What does winning get us?"

"Don't you know? If we win...we can get an extra order of fatty tuna sushi!"

"Fatty tuna...!"

Shiika's eyes lit up.

"Now then, first you'll introduce yourself according to the script I wrote, and while you're at it, sing a casual a cappella version of a song that's trending right now. Then you can easily grab yourself a whole heap of Impachi Live viewers! And after that...we feast! Mwah-ha-ha!"

"I'll do it...for fatty tuna..."

She clenched her tiny fists, motivated.

Come on, Shiika.

Show them the true talent of a singer who's a niche online sensation… Show them what you can really do!

◊ ◊ ◊

"What the…heck…?"

The following day. I was shocked and dumbfounded when I looked up the archives for the self-intro streams and saw the number of views and Likes. My hand slid limply from the safety strap, and I fell to my knees like soggy wakame.

Shiika leaned over to peer at my phone, which had fallen to the floor.

"Gak. Is it…fatty tuna?"

"Fatty tuna is out of the question."

"Perhaps we could still afford medium fatty tuna?"

"No."

"Oh dear…"

Her eyes, which had been shining innocently, suddenly lost their light and clouded over.

It must have been a shock. I could understand. I was shocked, too.

But my despondency only lasted for about a second.

"Wait a minute! How can that BE?!"

In an instant, my negative emotions escalated into anger, and I exploded.

Well, I mean, it didn't make sense. How could Shiika's I Tried Singing stream bring in a result like this?!

Incidentally, these were the numbers displayed on my phone.

[Views] 178 [Likes] 3 [Revenue] 0 yen
[Subscribers] 3

It couldn't possibly be worse.

Looking at the streams of other freshmen from Ryouran High School who posted under the same hashtag… Most of them had over two hundred views.

In other words, it wouldn't be an exaggeration to say that Shiika's stream had the lowest possible numbers.

She'd only gotten three Likes, so it was easy to tell who those Likes had come from.

I was one of them, so that meant she actually only had two real fans... But then, there's also the possibility that someone clicked out of habit or just did it randomly.

"Why...? Were the others super prodigies compared to Shiika...?"

I hurriedly put on my earphones that I plugged into my smartphone.

With a trembling thumb, I tapped one of our classmates' stream archive.

"Thank you sooo much for joining me for my first-ever stream!"

This was trash. Next.

"Okay, so now I'm going to try singing...you know the one! The song that broke records for the most consecutive weeks on the Royal Board ranking!"

Don't start your first stream by doing something completely unorthodox. Next.

"I challenged myself to eat everything on NackDonald's menu!"

That's got nothing to do with music! Next!

I swiped around with my thumb, checking out the streams of our classmates, but they were all complete garbage.

Many of them didn't seem related to music at all. How could Shiika's I Tried Singing stream lose to nonsense like this?

The two things these students had that Shiika lacked were the fact that they were able to project their voices and being clearly good-looking.

Mediocre content and singing ability aside, they had that celebrity aura.

I'd started looking at other low-ranked streams like Shiika's, but no doubt the high-ranking streams were much better in terms of looks and talent.

"I guess I'll do some research later when I have time... Ugh, watching them all is going to be such a hassle. Hey, maybe there's a ranking somewhere of students we should actually pay attention to... Hmm?"

"Gak, look. It's Mana."

"Oh yes, that's Akiba. What was she doing, streaming this morning?"

In the thumbnail that had caught my eye, the girl who had sat next to me yesterday—Mana Akihabara—was flashing a peace sign.

"If she's in the Music Department, that must mean she's also a music creator, huh."

"I'm looking forward to hearing Mana's sound. I want to listen to her."

"All right."

At Shiika's request, I put one of the earphones in her small ear.

Then I opened up Mana Akihabara's stream archive.

"Welcome to ManaMana's Channel for all things Ryouran High! Here, I rank streams and introduce noteworthy students who post with the Ryouran High School hashtag!"

"Isn't that a piggybacking business method?!"

"It wasn't a song... Oh. That's disappointing."

"Hmm, it seems there's a large discrepancy between top and bottom students this year. While the top level has a few actual prodigies, the middle tier is seriously thin on talent. Oh dear, this is quite terrible."

"She's criticizing the other students' streams... Who does she think she is?"

Unfortunately, Akiba's stream had far more views than Shiika's from the previous night.

Over one thousand views already. And it was an early-morning broadcast. It was likely to reach five thousand views today.

"Well, in a world where people seek out hashtags, there's a need for easy information, gathered in one channel..."

Oh, actually, this was exactly the kind of thing I was just looking for.

In fact, Akiba's summary was really useful. Just by skimming it, I was able to grasp the ability level of most of the Music Department students.

No surprises that Erio Shibuya was at the top. No wonder she was so arrogant in the classroom yesterday. She had the chops to back it up.

[Views] 304,860 [Likes] 9,830 [Revenue] 284,950 yen
[Subscribers] 46,000

Insanity. Even active professionals can't pull in those kinds of numbers.

Besides her self-intro stream, her content seemed to be I Tried Singing videos, like Shiika's.

"I want to hear this one."

"All right."

I closed Akiba's channel page to search for Erio Shibuya's archive.

Actually, I didn't even need to search.

Her channel had risen to the top of the home page, and her rank was soaring.

When I clicked on her first stream, the voice I heard produced such pressure that my ears popped. For a moment, I wondered what it was, but it was Erio Shibuya's voice. She started her stream with a greeting.

Her voice was also quite loud, which you'd expect from a singer.

It was loud, but it wasn't unpleasant. Her words carried in dulcet tones, and I found my eyes naturally drawn to the screen.

But Shiika seemed to have no interest in other people's boring self-introductions and impatiently tugged at my sleeve.

"Skip to the song."

"Okay. Um... Should be around here..."

I fast-forwarded until she started saying something like, *And now I shall sing...*

Then I pressed PLAY again.

What I heard was a clear whisper that almost seemed to tickle my eardrums with a feather.

Erio sang the trendy ballad beautifully with a delicate, innocent voice.

Yeah, she was incredibly good.

Honestly, though, I feel like Shiika is better. But that's only because Shiika is out of this world.

Erio's singing was at a professional level, no question about it. Compared to the other students' awful I Tried Singing videos from earlier, it was chalk and cheese. Like, if Erio was the beautiful Kaguya-hime from the fairy tale, then the other students were the turtles from the tale of Urashima Taro.

"...Hmm?"

Shiika tilted her head.

Something seemed to have caught her attention. She kept twisting her neck around.

"Hmm...?"

"What? Is something bothering you?"

"Hmm... It's something... I can't see it properly with earphones."

"Oh, right."

Shiika's synesthesia makes her see sounds as colors.

The easiest way for her to see them is to concentrate on live sound, right in front of her. But when there's a separation, the color becomes blurry and difficult to make out.

She'd picked up on something odd about Erio Shibuya's singing voice but wasn't able to identify what it was.

That feeling was probably unpleasant because Shiika had started shaking her head violently.

"Guh! Ugh! Guh!"

"Hey! Don't swing your long hair about! It's hitting me in the face."

"Can't...stand it... Ugh..."

"Stop, Shiika! Pwah! Your hair! It's getting in my mouth!"

But her long hair kept on slapping me, softly and mercilessly, until we got off the train.

Chapter 2:
Two Talents

On the second day of school, the atmosphere in the classroom was somewhat different.

Even though class was due to start soon, no one had their textbooks out. Instead, they were all talking about yesterday's streams. Incidentally, the textbooks that were delivered to us in advance of school starting were for basic subjects like Japanese, English, and math. There was nothing related to the performing arts.

When I asked what we'd be doing today, Mana Akihabara puffed out her chest and proudly explained it to me.

"Singing practice in the afternoon. Customized curriculum in the morning."

"Customized curriculum? Could you speak Japanese, please?"

"I am speaking Japanese… At this school, instead of everyone taking the same classes, students can decide for themselves what classes to take."

"Huh. So it's kind of like a university in that sense."

"There are some compulsory subjects that you absolutely have to take. Like, most of the music-related classes are compulsory for musicians. Writing lyrics, musical composition, vocal training, if there's a specific field you want to study more deeply, then you can take electives in those fields."

"I see. Can we take classes in other departments?"

When I read the pamphlet I received, it seemed that in addition to the Music Department, this school had various others related to the performing arts, like the Dance Department, the Fashion Department, the Variety Talent Department, and so on.

If we can choose our classes freely, then wouldn't it be possible to cross certain disciplines? That's what I was thinking when I asked that question, so when Akiba nodded, it looked like I'd hit the mark.

"Natch. It's a good idea, in fact, to get on good terms with kids from other departments, too. If you can make connections with students with promising futures, it might be to your advantage post-graduation."

"Now, that's forward-thinking. I envy your strong business spirit."

"Well, duh. Why'd you think I'm going to Ryouran in the first place? It's to become influential in the entertainment industry, of course."

"That's not the case for us."

Shiika, of course, was different. She had no interest in the entertainment world. But we were both very interested in the money she might be able to make there.

"I've drawn up a list of people to get close to. And I've researched which classes you should take if you wanted to become close with certain people. It's pay-per-view, of course. Mwah-ha-ha."

"Are you serious? You're trying way too hard to establish connections."

I was a little bit grossed out.

Looking at Akiba grinning away, phone in hand, a thought suddenly crossed my mind.

"Wait a minute, did you do some sort of calculation and decide to be friends with us based on the results...?"

"Oh, no. Certainly not. Never."

She was way too quick to deny that.

"What benefit is there for me to hang out with a local karaoke talent? I'm just chatting with you two because I think we'll get along."

"Because we're all unpopular dorks together?"

"Can you not lump me in with you like that? Anyway, it's not like you're a dork. Guys five times dorkier than you still manage to be cool if they put in just a little effort."

"Well, I'm not going to put in effort, so I guess we'll never know."

"Pipe down. I'm not going to share it with you. My list of movers and shakers, that is. Your future annual earnings can increase by several zeros depending on who you make connections with, you know. Such a shame; too bad for you."

"I'm sorry, I beg your pardon, I apologize! Please share your wisdom with this lowly worm!"

I apologized, in as many ways as I could think of.

Akiba seemed mollified by my groveling, and said that since I insisted, she'd explain.

"First, we have to start with Io Kanda. The top student in the Talent Department. Good looks. To get the required level of muscle tone needed for her acting performance, she takes the Basics of Strength Training class every year. Although it only earns you a couple of credits, anyone can take that class, from first-years to third-years. Even people who've already earned the credit for that class can keep taking it each year, since it gets them in the habit of exercising using the school's gym," Akiba said, looking smug.

No wonder Io's the top of her department. Her approach to her acting is on another level.

"Next, we have the top student in the Fashion Department, Azusa Harajuku. Good looks. Her talent is already drawing attention in Europe. A supernova in the world of fashion designers under her dark persona, AZU. Apparently, she plans to take the Designing Spaces and Colors class, so I intend to take that, too. It'll be useful when it comes to staging live music events, as well, see."

I did see. I thought music was music, and fashion was fashion, but the two intersected in surprising ways.

"Next is Tatsuki Ootsuka, the top student in first-year Dance. Good looks. Draws attention as the gifted hip-hop dancer Ryuzetsuran and destroys challengers in knockout dance battles. Apparently she's into all aspects of hip-hop culture, so she's bound to take the Hip-hop Music class."

She destroys challengers in knockout dance battles? What is she, some kind of Pokémon master? What's wrong with this school?

"Those are the people you should keep an eye on from other departments. Now, within the Music Department, we have Erio Shibuya, Nokia Komae... But since we're in the same department, you won't be able to avoid being around them."

"So those are the five I should be aware of, huh. But there's one thing that bothers me. Mind if I ask?"

"Go on."

"Why did you add 'good looks' to your description of each person?"

"Because it's vitally important. I'm not exaggerating when I say it's an absolute requirement to be at the top."

"Guh..."

It came as no surprise to hear, but yeah... This school seemed to base everything on physical appearances.

"How do you go about customizing your own curriculum?"

"Gakuto, were you not listening to the teachers at all? Here, I'll show you. Get your phone out."

Access the Ryouran High portal site via smartphone.

Log in using your student ID number (apparently, we use the same ID and password as the Impachi Live account we created yesterday) and tap CURRICULUM to display the timetable.

Looking around, I realized the other students were leaving the classroom, chatting, and basically doing whatever they wanted.

"Looks like everyone's free to do anything in the mornings."

"Right. Starting today, for a week, we can take all kinds of classes on a trial basis. Then we choose a selection of our favorites to make a customized curriculum, and then starting next week, all students will take classes according to their own personalized timetable."

"I see. What will you take, Shiika? For nonmusic classes, I mean."

Thinking what a novel system it was, I spoke to Shiika, who was on the other side.

Shiika stopped staring blankly at Erio Shibuya across the room and turned to me, looking sluggish.

"What are you talking about?"

"Weren't you listening? What elective classes are you going to take?"

"Whichever. As long as I can hear some nice sounds, I'll be satisfied."

"Can't you try to be more involved?"

"You're the one doing the decision-making. Do it for me."

She tossed her phone over.

Don't toss it!

Well, no doubt Shiika would end up taking the same classes as me anyway, so it wasn't really an issue.

I would fulfil my duties as manager, of course.

Even so, I didn't have any particular classes that I wanted to take, so I just decided it'd be fine to go with the same curriculum as Akiba.

◊ ◊ ◊

At lunchtime, Shiika, Akiba, and I headed to the cafeteria.

The cafeteria was in a large building a short distance from the classroom.

It was spacious, about 150 meters, with room for around a hundred people. There was even seating on the wooden terrace outside. It looked more like some stylish resort restaurant than a school cafeteria.

It was packed, bustling with students. The atmosphere was buzzing, and as someone who didn't like crowds, I felt somewhat uncomfortable.

We managed to secure a table.

No doubt that was only because we'd gotten there a little early. Without even taking any trial classes, we spent the morning customizing our curriculum.

When I thought that it was probably going to get even more crowded than this, to the point where we'd have trouble getting seats…it was daunting.

"…Too many people. Feel dizzy…"

"You said it. Starting tomorrow, let's skip the cafeteria and buy our lunches at the convenience store."

"It's just a school cafeteria. What are you trembling about?"

Akiba didn't seem bothered at all.

Her drab appearance put her in the same basket as us, but no doubt, her ability to adapt to situations was far more advanced than ours.

...Or maybe us former shut-ins were just that inferior.

"And what's with that lunch? What are we, in prison?"

"Ah, that..."

Shiika and I both had only a single bowl on our trays.

We had just plain udon in a simple soup with one slice of deep-fried tofu on top. And that was it.

"Udon. With basically no toppings. What is this, some kind of diet?"

"Gak... Gak, this is too much to bear..."

With her shoulders slumped, Shiika poked at the deep-fried tofu with the tips of her chopsticks.

"I don't like it, either. But it can't be helped."

"Ha-ha-ha! Because Shiika's stream didn't take off at all!"

"Don't laugh... I never thought it would end up like this, either."

"But I was told that I could eat sushi every day..."

I mean, I wanted to treat Shiika to her heart's content, too, of course I did...

But based on the results of yesterday's stream, I couldn't exactly hope for a fancy lifestyle for us.

We needed to cut back on our expenses, or we'd be bankrupt in no time at all.

"Aw, poor little lambs. Now look, kindhearted Mana will give you some of hers."

Saying that, Akiba picked up two stems of broccoli from the bowl of salad on her tray using her chopsticks and dropped one into each of our bowls.

Don't put broccoli in people's udon. It's so obvious you're just getting rid of foods you don't like.

"Hey, that's a pretty extravagant lunch."

Akiba's lunch was quite the spread.

She had butter rice, beef skirt steak, mashed potatoes, and a colorful vegetable salad.

It looked absolutely delicious. I could feel myself salivating.

"Hee-hee. This is the lunch of champions."

"Darn it, Akiba... You make easy money just uploading roundups of the other students' stream numbers and ranking them. But what is it that you actually do, besides that?"

"I compose."

"Show us your songs, then."

"Ah, nope, no thanks. Don't think the work of a creative is all that easy. It's no simple thing, creating a song, you know."

"Then when will you release your first song publicly?"

"Sometime, I guess?"

"Sometime? ...Come on, now."

"Hmm, how can I put this...? The god of creation has yet to bless me. If He decides to descend from the heavens with an amazing concept for me, then I guess I'd be fine to go public with it anytime."

That sounded like the kind of excuse given by those who went their whole lives never actually creating anything.

But I didn't say that out loud. I just thought it. I wouldn't want to go hurting her pride.

"Well, don't look so down. You were scouted because of Shiika's voice, right? That must mean her singing ability is pretty good, yeah?"

"Did you see it? Shiika's stream?"

"Natch. I can't very well do a roundup of all first-years without checking out each stream. I even gave her a Like, since we're friends. You're welcome."

"What...the...?"

I was shocked and dumbfounded by Akiba's casual, throwaway remark.

Akiba looked confused.

"Wh-what's wrong? Your face... You already looked like you were going through a great depression, but now you're practically spiraling like a deflated balloon."

"One of our three Likes was...you?"

"Huh?"

"One was me. One was you, Akiba. Shiika's not the type to Like her own videos, which means we only have one genuine fan. Ah-ha. Ha-ha-ha…"

"Er, hello? Earth to Gakuto? …No good; his eyes look dead."

"Ha-ha, ha-ha-ha. This udon is so good. This deep-fried tofu is, like, a luxury food. Ah-ha-ha-ha."

Yikes. I was full-on bawling.

Shiika's vocal ability, which I'd been so proud of, was, in Akiba's words…only "pretty good."

I'd always thought Shiika's singing was god-tier. Perhaps it was just rose-colored glasses, worn by an elder brother with an extreme sister complex?

Now I was starting to worry about the afternoon's classes.

If she was directly compared against the other students in terms of musical performance, I might have to confront the fact that Shiika's talent was only mediocre.

I thought she was a genius, so I felt confident before, but now… Now everything had been turned upside down.

Ohhh, I couldn't take the anxiety.

Wanting some warmth and reassurance, I reached for the head of my cute little sister, who was slurping noodles next to me with a blank expression. As if she were a stuffed animal, I caressed her soft hair, which held the natural scent of a sun-dried futon.

With one hand, she slapped me.

"Not now. Don't touch me. I can't eat if you do that."

"Let me at least feel your warmth…"

"Hey, hey, don't go doing anything crazy like dropping out in the first month. We're friends, aren't we?"

"Akiba… Would you miss us if we were gone?"

So warm.

Self-centered, self-righteous, doesn't write songs or do anything by herself… Ah, when I think of her that way, she's a good egg after all!

"If the friends I've chosen disappear all at once, I'll be alone. Don't quit until I've had the chance to make other friends, at least."

"You really only think about yourself, don't you? Ah, it's sort of refreshing."

But my anxiety about the afternoon's classes only continued to grow.

◊ ◊ ◊

In the afternoon, we had a Vocal Basics class.

The studio for vocal lessons on the third floor of the school building was packed with about forty students from the Music Department.

The flooring was smooth, polished, and reflected the light. A huge mirror took up the entire wall on one side (apparently, this is called a continuous mirror). There was all the equipment necessary for music lessons: microphones, keyboards, sound equipment, and so on.

But today it seemed we'd only be using a plain whiteboard.

The students were sitting on the floor anyhow, listening to the teacher (who, for some reason, had an Afro).

By the way, it seemed to be a Ryouran High rule that no matter how students behaved in class, teachers were to never intervene. Whether the students paid attention to him or not, Mr. Afro didn't seem to care.

Honestly, it helped me out a lot. I mean, I had no intention of seriously taking these classes.

I mean, right now, I was in the far corner of the classroom, resting against the railing that was in front of the mirror. Phone out, totally slacking off.

Judging from the smattering of words that I could hear, it seemed to be a simple lecture on the mechanics of vocalization. I wasn't expecting a full-on vocal lesson or anything, since it was only the first day, but this was even more boring than I'd anticipated.

The teacher had drawn the upper half of the human body on the whiteboard and was painstakingly explaining how the movements of the lungs, throat, airway, and skeleton were connected to vocalization.

No doubt it was important stuff, but it must have been boring to anyone who had even a basic grasp of how vocals work... And yes, Shiika was fast asleep next to me.

It wasn't just Shiika, either.

Most of the students, including Erio Shibuya, seemed to be off in their own little worlds.

"Can I stand here?"

"Huh?"

Someone must have approached me because I heard a voice to one side.

Lifting my head, I saw a guy with red hair.

It was the guy I'd noticed in the classroom on the first day, one of the ones who stuck out.

He was the one saying those conceited things to the girls… Nokia Komae. Now he was standing next to me, leaning his back against the mirror.

"You didn't even wait for me to say yes, so why ask?"

"Ah-ha-ha. ☆ Well, I knew you wouldn't say no, so what's the harm?"

"Uh… Sure…"

Here's another one who seems to be very self-assured.

Komae smiled, and it was the smile of someone who'd never known rejection in all his sixteen years of life.

"It's unusual, isn't it, for a brother and sister to enter the school together? And you must have had to repeat a year or two before getting in. Now that's tenacity."

"No, you're totally wrong. I'm something like Shiika's manager. I only entered this school because of special circumstances. I said that during my self-introduction, if you were listening."

"Ah yes, the self-introduction. I thought you were mumbling something. So that's what you were saying, then?"

"…"

Now I knew I'd messed up my self-intro for sure.

I'd introduced myself with a defensive smile and made sure not to think about it too much. If I didn't look, it wouldn't hurt—Schrödinger style! Was I screwing up? No way to tell, so what did it matter? But according to this guy, I'd made a fool of myself after all. Ugh, I wanted to die.

"…Please kill me."

"No way; I don't want to get involved in any scandals."

That's his only issue with that request?

"Actually, I want to confirm something. Do you mind?"

"What is it?"

"Do I need her manager's permission if I want to seduce Shiika?"

"…What?"

Immediately, I became serious.

Komae continued rambling on, oblivious to the fact that I was now planning how to murder him with my bare hands.

"Shiika's no amateur, is she?"

"Huh?"

I wasn't expecting him to say that, and now he had my interest.

"What gives you that impression?"

"I saw her stream yesterday. Her presentation wasn't polished at all. I just didn't get that spark from her."

"Wow, you sure don't sugarcoat things, do you?"

"But her singing ability. Now, that was the one thing that was pro level. She's very uneven, isn't she?"

"You sound very confident in your appraisals."

I felt like needling him.

I disliked people who looked down on others. Now that I'd been confronted by the stark reality of Shiika's viewing numbers, his compliments sounded hollow.

"She's a ball of nerves. But I gave her a Like, so give me some credit. I'm a fan, here."

"You gave her a Like? Hold on. Are you serious?"

"Yeah. Here's the evidence."

Komae showed me his phone. Under his Liked videos, I spotted Shiika's.

I quickly checked Shiika's channel. Her number of Likes hadn't increased. It still stood at three.

Wait. In other words, the people who Liked the stream were…Akiba, Komae, and me.

The mysterious third person, who could have been the only genuine fan, turned out to be another classmate. This was terrible. Our careers at Ryouran High were over. Farewell, sushi. Farewell, happy unemployed life.

"Hello? Anyone in there?"

"...What?!"

"Get a grip, manager. This is no time to be taking a break from reality."

"After decimating me, you're going to lecture me on how to react? You've got some nerve."

"Why are you so hostile? I mean, I'm on your side, here. Ah, whatever."

Komae turned around and looked in the mirror.

Gazing at himself, he continued talking as he began fixing his hair.

"You shouldn't turn your nose up at being stylish. If you want to get results in this school, good looks are more important than anything else."

"Looks are all you need, huh? This is supposed to be the Music Department. Can't we evaluate based on, I don't know, singing ability?"

"Well, that's the bare minimum requirement to get in. Anyway, I'm not just talking about physical looks."

"What do you mean?"

"Think it over for yourself."

What the heck was with this guy?

Did he think he was cool? Giving "meaningful" advice like this?

I glared at him in defiance, but he didn't seem like he was going to bother explaining himself after all.

Once he was done fiddling with his hair...

"Show me this isn't all that you have to offer. And say hi to Shiika for me."

With that, he exited the studio.

...Er, class is still in session? He was just a blatant slacker, wasn't he? Although, at this school, as long as you abide by the rules, students are technically free to come and go.

Though I didn't exactly have the moral high ground when it came to being a slacker to be able to make these comments about another person.

◊ ◊ ◊

After school, in the classroom, I just said it straight.

"Let's do a transformation, Shiika."

"...Like a magical girl transformation?"

"No, no. Not some fantasy one. A real-life transformation."

In other words, become more fashionable, I said.

"Fashion...? It's too much of a hassle."

"But if you want to get more views, you can't stay the way you are. You have to change! Right, Akiba?!"

"What? Are you talking to me?"

Akiba, who was just about to stand up to go home, with her school bag on her shoulder, turned around with a start.

No doubt she sensed trouble in the air and tried to escape, but I couldn't let her do that.

"Of course I'm talking to you. You're going to help, too."

"D-don't get me involved in this. I don't want to deal with it."

"Please! You need to know who's on your side and who isn't in order to do battle, right? You know every student at Ryouran High! With your keen eye, we can figure out the exact type of fashion that's needed to win!"

"Gah, I don't wanna."

"Don't say that; you're our friend, aren't you? I'll do anything! What do you say?"

"Hmm... You really will do anything, then?"

"Of course, I reserve the right to turn down any crazy requests. Don't go discounting the Japanese constitution, now."

"There's nothing I really want from you anyway..."

"But you're a composer. It would be to your advantage to do a collaboration with a vocalist. Shiika's popularity, or lack thereof, should be of major concern to you, too, Akiba."

"Oh, blegh. Gakuto, you're sharper than you look..."

"That's the spirit! So we're doing this, then?!"

"Yeek!"

I'd backed Akiba up against the wall. With a small thud, her shoulders hit the wall, and she slid down to the floor.

"I'll... I'll cooperate..."

"Okay, the deal is done! School sucks, but friends are the best!"

Shazam! I struck a pose. It was the kind of pose you might come up with if you danced all night and were completely sleep-deprived.

It was really nice to have someone I could rely on.

Frankly, there was no way Shiika and I could figure out what to do about her appearance all by ourselves. No doubt, if this was a shounen manga, we'd earn abilities through hard work, but I'm not that diligent. I'm lazy, but if I can get decent results without having to work hard, then that's what I'd rather do.

"So it's decided. Don't go running off, now."

"Agh..."

I grabbed Shiika's shoulder as she tried to sidle past me.

Realizing that she'd missed her chance to escape, Shiika looked defeated, and Akiba looked dismayed. I turned to them both and gave them wide grins.

"Come on! Let's get this after-school fun started!"

◊ ◊ ◊

The downtown area is just a short walk from Ryouran High.

The crowds of people swarming, like ants to ice cream that had fallen on the ground, made me feel nauseous. Still, I endured it for the sake of views, Likes, and money. Shiika and I marched through the streets.

Only Akiba looked calm and slipped skillfully among people with her eyes glued to her phone.

Hey, looking at your phone while walking is dangerous. Tsk, the youth these days...

...Oh wait, she's only two years younger than me.

"So much walking... I'm tired."

"Hey, where are you taking us?"

Using Shiika's complaint as pretext, I called out to Akiba.

She looked up from her phone before responding.

"Cosmetics store."

"Cosmetics? You mean like makeup?"

"Yes. Before clothes, we have to start by constructing the right kind of face."

"Huh. I had no idea you knew so much about makeup."

At first glance, she looked like she had nothing on, so I assumed she didn't care about stuff like that.

Could this be the natural makeup look you always hear about? A friend on *EPEX* (a total online creeper) told me there are girls in this world who are absolute masters at makeup, and their specialty is making it appear as if they aren't even wearing it at all. These days, there are so many girls who try to look the same, and some are complete catfishes—you can't even trust your own eyes anymore.

Ah, so Akiba, too, is a master at that kind of makeup, I thought.

"Nope. I don't wear makeup or stuff like that."

"You don't?! Hey, hey, HEY! Then how the heck are you gonna choose makeup for Shiika, then?"

"Oh, pipe down. I'm looking it up on my phone, see?"

She showed me her phone. It looked like she was on some kind of chat forum for girls.

There were a ton of posts on things women tend to be interested in, like health and love stuff. It seemed like you could post questions and even answer other people's inquiries as well.

Akiba had posted a question in the beauty subsection: "Can anyone tell me what kind of good, cheap makeup would suit me?"

She'd described Shiika's features in the post, and now it seemed that more knowledgeable ladies were posting responses.

"But these people responding are just online amateurs, aren't they? Are you sure we should take their advice?"

"What gives you the right to make fun of amateurs? Compared to the girls who are posting here, we're beneath them!"

"Well, you've got a point there!"

Her logic was bulletproof.

Sorry for doubting you with such arrogance, kind internet anons.

"I've already gotten a response."

"That was fast!"

"The power of the internet is truly terrifying... Let's see. Aha. Yes, indeed."

I craned my neck to peer at Akiba's screen as she nodded.

I couldn't read the whole thing, of course, but I could make out a few bullet points. It was stuff about how to apply makeup in ways to bring out Shiika's features, the kinds of tools we'd need, and recommendations for makeup brands. Other commenters would add their know-how as well, and every time we refreshed, there were more comments. There was even someone who kindly posted a step-by-step guide to makeup application, with attached photos. In no time at all, this one post had turned into a veritable textbook of information.

It truly is terrifying, this modern online society we live in.

Suddenly, I noticed someone had posed a question directly to the OP.

"Are you a student, wearing makeup for the first time? If you don't understand the basics yet, you might want to learn how to prep your eyes first."

Someone else had responded to that.

"It might be difficult to give advice, since the shape of one's eyes and their bone structure varies from person to person. Would you mind uploading a picture of just your eyes?"

And so the conversation continued.

Akiba must have read that part because she muttered something like, "They've got a point there."

She pointed her phone at Shiika.

"Let me take a picture of your eyes."

"No!"

Realizing that Akiba was about to lift up her bangs, Shiika pressed down on them with both hands.

"Don't make such a fuss! This is necessary."

"Hmph!"

Shiika twisted away, and Akiba tussled with her, trying to move her hands aside.

They both had about the same amount of upper-body strength. If this continued, we wouldn't be getting anywhere.

"Shiika, please. For the sake of our livelihoods."

For the sake of humankind...would be the cool, hero-esque line there. But what came out of my mouth was a phrase born from the desperation of an ordinary man who just wanted to pay rent.

"I don't wanna."

"Gah! Okay, desperate times call for desperate measures. Here... Devil horns!"

I pinched my thumb, middle, and ring fingers together, with my index finger and pinkie sticking straight up like devil horns.

Then I waved them in front of Shiika's face.

"What are you doing, Gakuto?"

"Just watch."

While Akiba looked on with a funny expression, I continued to wave my devil horns around. Shiika's eyes followed them from left to right. Letting go of her bangs, Shiika made her own devil horns, bringing them up to bump against mine, like giving a small kiss.

I yelped:

"Now!"

"Oh, right. Yes, great photo op!"

Akiba swept Shiika's bangs aside and snapped a pic of her eyes using her phone camera.

Shiika glared at me, her eyes filled with resentment.

"...That's no fair. You fooled me by using the devil horns against me."

"It's for the sake of your views—and our living expenses. Please forgive me."

"I will never be lured by your devil horns again, Gak."

"Devil horns."

I lifted them up in front of Shiika's eyes again, and without hesitation, she made her own, and our devil horns had another small kiss.

"…! Darn it! My hand just moved on its own!"

"Conditioned behavior from childhood… Amazing."

It was something silly we'd come up with in our family to soothe Shiika whenever she started whining. The fact that it still worked on her as an almost grown adult was both convenient and a little bit creepy.

She quickly posted the photo to be assessed by those online anons, and Akiba sighed with amazement.

"You know, for a brother and sister, you're really weird."

◊ ◊ ◊

After buying most of the necessary things we needed like makeup, beauty tools, and new clothes, we headed to our place.

Luckily, the closest station to our house was only a few stops away from the apartment where Akiba lived by herself. So it wasn't too far for her.

A crumbling apartment building in the suburbs. Ivy overgrown on the walls. The second floor.

The Ikebukuro siblings lived in a simple two-room, one-kitchen apartment.

Compared to Ryouran High, with its glittering, castle-ballroom ambience, this was more like the house where Cinderella lived. A shabby girl covered in ashes after the magical spell had worn off.

But for Shiika and me, a simple, ordinary place like this was far more comfortable.

"Gakuto. You've got a nerve, inviting a girl over to a decrepit place like this."

But Akiba didn't seem to like our place very much and started complaining from the moment she walked through the door.

"What do you mean, a place like this? We live here, thank you very much."

"If you want respect, you need a certain standard of living! Look at this! Don't you have any pride?"

Akiba pointed at the comics, documents, and empty cardboard boxes scattered on the floor.

Sure, it might be a little messy, but…is it really worth mentioning?

"Don't look so shocked! This place is a pigsty!"

"Th-that's very rude of you to say. Look, we clean up our perishable waste and make sure to dispose of it on schedule. It doesn't even smell… Or at least, it shouldn't…"

"That's your criteria for a pleasant home? Wait, you mean to say you do actually clean this place?"

"Of course! Once a month! We never skip it."

"Once a month?! You need to do it once a week at least! Better yet, every day!"

"That's too much trouble!"

"Are you even human beings?"

While Akiba complained, I hustled her into the living room.

We ate our meals in our own rooms each day, so the low table didn't get much use. Piled on top of it was an assortment of random, unidentifiable things. Like a bulldozer, I swept it all onto the carpet, then laid out the bag of odd cosmetics and beauty tools we'd bought.

"You can sit anywhere you like, on the sofa or on the floor."

"I'll take the sofa… There's no clean space on the floor…"

"Our low table!"

While Akiba lowered herself onto the sofa with a disgusted look, Shiika slipped under our low table.

"All right then, Akiba. It's all up to you. Shiika, turn your face toward her."

"All right. Here."

Shiika did as instructed, after plopping her chin down on the table.

Akiba made a very unpleasant face.

"Are you even willing to do this at all?"

"Of course we are. Why do you think we brought you here? You think shut-ins invite strangers into their home? You wouldn't even be here if we weren't expecting big things from you!"

"Just so many stupid remarks, one after another... Gah, whatever. I'm a beginner, too, just so you know, so don't go expecting too much from me."

"Don't worry. You know more than anyone else here."

Alas, Shiika was right.

With a sigh of resignation, Akiba immediately set to work, phone in one hand and the makeup tools we'd bought in the other.

"Er, let's see. First, break down the components that make a quote-unquote beautiful woman. Beautiful skin, size of nose, double eyelids, eye shape, brow thickness, chin shape. Compare your features to those of a beautiful woman and work on the parts that don't fit... Gosh, this sounds like such a hassle."

Mumbling to herself, Akiba continued perusing the beauty advice given by the online anons.

"For now, let's start with the skin. Excuse me."

"Mmn."

Akiba leaned forward and touched Shiika's face.

"Apparently, rough skin is no good, but... Would you say this is rough? It seems nice to me. But then, what do I know?"

"Ah, that's my little sister for you. Of course her skin's beautiful. She's fearsome!"

"Oh, shut up, you sister-loving freak. Hmm, let's start by washing your face."

"Mmn... Pahhh."

Shiika screwed her eyes shut as Akiba splashed water on her face.

Then she wriggled like a dog getting a bath as Akiba dried her face with a tissue.

"Hee! That tickles."

"Quit squirming. Hey, freak with a sister complex. Hold her down."

"Ah... Okay."

I did as instructed and grabbed Shiika's shoulders.

She kept on squirming, but since she was wedged under the low table, she wasn't able to put up much resistance.

After that, things went surprisingly smoothly.

After washing the face came skin prep with toner and something called skin milk.

Then make the skin glow with a makeup base and finish it off with a powder foundation.

A touch of eye shadow, enough to go unnoticed.

Shiika has slightly droopy eyes, so to give them some more charisma and impact, Akiba used brushes and eyeliner to make them appear slightly upturned at the corners.

It was a bit too much, perhaps, for a high school student's daily look, but we couldn't neglect adding color to her cheeks and lips. We had to be conscious of how it looked when she was streaming.

Akiba took care of Shiika's makeup one step at a time, very methodically, consulting her phone the whole time. After a while, Shiika seemed to become more comfortable with the process and began to relax. Before long, she even seemed to be somewhat enjoying the attention.

As a finishing touch, Akiba pinned Shiika's bangs back so her face would be on full display.

And then it was time to appraise Shiika's finished look…

"Wow…"

"Hmm, it's not bad at all. I think I did a pretty good job, actually!"

I was impressed, and Akiba indulged in some self-praise.

I held up the hand mirror (purchased today, of course… We certainly didn't have anything fancy like that at home) in front of Shiika's face.

"Huh…?"

Gazing at herself in the mirror, Shiika's aura took on a unique color that deepened in intensity.

What was she thinking about? Her expression was vague, emotionless. Her mouth was half-open, and her lips were glistening. She poked her reflection in the mirror, as if to confirm that what she was seeing was real.

Was she stunned to see herself wearing makeup for the first time in her life? Or was she stunned by the extent of her own latent potential? Or perhaps she was simply overwhelmed by her own beauty?

Akiba and I waited for her impressions when Shiika finally found her voice.

"I don't really remember what I looked like before this, to be honest."

"That's what you have to say? Seriously?"

It felt like missing a step going down the stairs. It wasn't that Shiika was stunned, or admiring her own beauty, or anything like that. She just paused because she thought, *Wait, but what did I look like before…?* It was a typical ditzy Shiika response, but even though she was my own sister, I had to say…"Come on, now."

"Come to think of it, you never really looked at yourself in the mirror when you were a shut-in, did you? And even when we started going to school, I was the one who mainly helped you get ready."

"Eugh, seriously? I knew your private life had to be quirky, but this… Gakuto, you seriously take care of her to that extent?"

Akiba frowned.

Shiika responded with no hint of guilt, as if it was all just par for the course.

"Yeah. I leave everything to Gak. I never even check the mirror."

"Insane boy and girl. What a disturbing pairing. Definitely odd."

"A five-seven-five syllable rhythm. Pretty. Sounds nice and crisp to the ear. Good job."

"Uh, you don't need to praise me on sentence structure."

Akiba looked annoyed when Shiika flashed her a thumbs-up.

Shiika seldom complimented people on their sounds. But Akiba had no way of knowing that this was high praise. If I took the trouble to explain, perhaps she'd be pleased. But I couldn't be bothered, so I decided not to.

Akiba sighed and reached for an unopened package.

"After the makeup is finished, next we need to fix your hair, then pick an outfit to match… Although I guess we don't really need to worry about that today."

"Why not?"

"Most people watch live streams on their phones for convenience, and it's standard for the angle to be a little closer. On a TV screen, for example, you need to factor in your entire body based on the camera shot, but if you're just aiming to get views, then looks—by which I mean, your face—are all you need."

"Really? I feel like I often see streams and videos that show the whole body."

"Sure, if it's a dance video or something fashion-related like a look book. That kind of content is all about the full-body shot. But for more chatty ones or I Tried Singing…videos, then there's no need to show the whole body."

"Huh. I see."

Wow, Akiba sure knows a lot. She's not just some bandit who earns money off the back of other people's popularity. She actually does her research.

"Well anyway, I'm heading home now. I'm exhausted."

"Thank you, Akiba."

"Thaaanks."

Shiika dragged out the vowel. She waved her hand, a gesture that may have appeared lackluster and dismissive, but it was actually just a lack of muscle tone that made her motions sluggish. Shiika, herself, was genuinely grateful.

"Would you like something to eat before you go home? Let us offer you something to say thanks."

"Hmm, should I take you up on that offer? What have you got to eat, by the way?"

"Seafood flavor and chili tomato flavor, whichever you prefer. I've also got instant udon, the red one and the green one."

"Instant ramen?! You're not gonna cook?!"

"I can't cook. Anyway, we don't even have any fresh produce here. We don't even have a knife. Or a cutting board."

We'd never use that kind of thing anyway.

"And yet you offer to treat me to food?! Ah, whatever. I'll eat once I get home. Don't worry about it."

"Oh, okay. Well, see you tomorrow. At school, right?"

"Later... Oh, I almost forgot."

Waving her hand listlessly, Akiba, who was heading to the front door, stopped and turned around.

"Don't forget to remove your makeup after the stream."

And with that as her parting remark, she left.

Honestly...she was a big help.

When I looked it up later, I discovered that you have to wash makeup off afterward. Neither Shiika nor I, with zero concept of makeup, would have thought to do that.

It felt like we'd been benefiting from Akiba's help in one way or another the entire day.

Incidentally, Shiika's stream that night was an immediate success.

[Views] 1,328 [Likes] 105 [Revenue] 0 yen
[Subscribers] 79 people

On the first day, we got only 178 views for the evening's stream, but by the time Shiika was done, we'd crossed the one thousand mark.

We also had over one hundred Likes, which was excellent. We hadn't made any revenue, but when I thought back on the devastation I'd felt over the first round's results, I realized I couldn't expect too much.

There weren't a lot of comments, but there were a decent number.

You're cute, I like your voice, you're good at singing, I'll subscribe, and so on. I was relieved to see so many positive comments.

To tell the truth, after our experiences as Seeker, I was worried that malicious commenters might pop up. I was ready to delete any cruel comments using my admin privileges, but luckily, those concerns went unfounded.

Maybe there were just fewer haters on Impachi Live. Or perhaps Shiika hadn't gotten enough views yet to attract the attention of haters? It was hard to pin down the reason, but either way, I was glad tonight went off without a hitch.

Still, compared to Erio Shibuya, sitting at over three hundred thousand views, we were small fry.

But even the longest journey started with a single step. All we had to do was slowly gain views going forward.

I was practically drooling, dreaming of a safe and stable unemployed life. I felt a tug at my sleeve. It was Shiika. She had just finished streaming, and her eyes were sparkling.

"Gak. Can we get tuna? Fatty tuna?"

"Sorry, that's out of the question."

"D'oh…"

"D'oh? What are you, some old guy?"

Even though our numbers had increased, we were still barely above the bottom of the pile. I actually didn't know how the number of views correlated to the amount of living expenses we could earn, but I knew I wouldn't feel secure until we broke into the top level, with more than fifty thousand views.

If we got carried away and went out eating fatty tuna now, we'd just be digging our own graves with chopsticks.

Being cautious was of the utmost importance.

◊ ◊ ◊

The following day. The first-year Music Department classroom at Ryouran High was buzzing with a strange energy.

When we entered the classroom, the noise grew louder, and curious glances were directed at us.

They were staring at…me. Yeah, right. They were staring at Shiika, beside me. No doubt unaware of all this attention from her classmates, Shiika wandered airily across the room, yawning sleepily.

I looked toward our desks. Akiba was in the same seat as yesterday. Noticing us, she beckoned us over. There was a phone and pencil case placed on the two seats alongside her. It looked like she'd saved seats for us.

I grabbed Shiika and pulled her close to me, interrupting her dubious manner of walking. As we approached Akiba, she greeted me with a wide grin.

"You did it, Gakuto. Everyone's talking about Shiika this morning."

"Shiika? Why?"

"Because they saw the stream last night, duh!"

"For real?!"

"For real."

I was excited and felt a flood of emotions. This was an unexpected development. For better or worse. I felt a hot mass swell up in my stomach, as if my whole body was filled with hot magma. The heat made me a little dizzy and slightly nauseous.

Everyone was looking at Shiika because of the results of her stream. That was a good thing. Logically, I knew that.

Unfortunately, I'm a total shut-in. And unlike Shiika, with her genius-level talent and total disregard for other people's opinions, I'm an ordinary guy. As such, I didn't like people looking at me. Whether it was good or bad attention, getting it in real life and offline… It didn't feel great.

"…Gulp."

"You okay? You look deathly pale."

"Ah, yeah. I'm fine. I just wasn't expecting this kind of reaction, that's all."

"Tsk, see, this is why you're such a pair of amateurs. How can someone with dreams of eventual stardom crumple in the face of a little attention?"

"I don't have dreams of eventual stardom."

I'm just the manager. The guy behind the curtain.

More precisely, I want to be a self-employed manager. To be a hired manager at an entertainment agency sounds like a lot of work, and I don't want to work.

"I didn't realize that yesterday's live stream alone would attract so much attention."

"Increasing the number of views by a factor of ten is actually really rare."

"Is it?"

"Yeah. And I think the reason why she's getting so much attention comes down to the fact that she's seriously cute."

"Even though she's not wearing makeup to school today?"

"Zzz... Zzz..."

I glanced over and saw Shiika already asleep with her cheek against the desk.

Not a hint of makeup, unlike during her live stream. Her bangs weren't pulled back now. They were hanging all over her face.

We had the stuff at home now, but neither Shiika nor I had any makeup application skills. Neither did we have the motivation to learn. Without Akiba, we couldn't re-create that same look.

Why don't you do some research on your phone and do it yourself, you may ask. Well, it's beyond me. Akiba was able to do it because she has this knack for gathering knowledge about other people. It's impossible for a normal beginner to suddenly be able to apply a perfect face of makeup.

Also, Shiika didn't even like having her bangs up at home, let alone at school.

She would have been exposed to a variety of sounds that were either too visible to her or uncomfortable to experience.

Our classmates continued to gossip, but nobody spoke to us directly.

Even in a specialized education facility like this one, some things never change. I got the slight impression that they were mocking us.

Fortunately, though, most of the gossip seemed to be positive.

Or so I thought...

"Yo, Gakuto."

Only one person actually spoke to me outright.

Red hair, handsome face, clean-cut. The good-looking playboy, Nokia Komae.

"I knew my hunch about her wasn't off the mark."

"Oh, now that she's getting a bit popular, you're going to crow about being an early adopter? Just so you know, we weren't influenced by you in any way."

"I know that. I figured you'd find the right path sooner or later by yourself."

"Can you stop sounding so high-and-mighty? It's really, really irritating."

"Ha-ha. You're harsh, Gakuto."

Komae shrugged and smiled. It was exactly that kind of attitude that ticked me off, but apparently he wasn't even aware of it.

Without trying to hide my displeasure, I decided to find out what this guy was up to.

"So what do you want?"

"I wanted to say hello to the beautiful diva."

Winking, Komae leaned down and got on eye level with Shiika, who was still asleep. He rapped on the desk with his fingertips.

"Shiika. Sorry to interrupt you when you're snoozing so adorably, but would you mind waking up? Perhaps you need a wake-up kiss first?"

"Hey! What are you playing at?"

I grabbed Komae by the shoulder and yanked him back.

Trying to hit on a guy's sister right in front of him... What are you trying to pull here? That's what I was thinking as I glared at him.

Without breaking his easygoing demeanor, Komae leaned closer to Shiika. *No way, buddy,* I thought, tugging him back again, but years of being a shut-in had left me with weak noodle arms.

We kept pushing and pulling, neither of us getting anywhere.

"Mmn... Huh?"

Shiika stirred.

Slowly, she raised her head, looking annoyed.

Rubbing her eyes, she squinted at me and Komae as we continued to tussle.

Making eye contact with Shiika, Komae grinned brightly.

"Good morning, Princess. I saw your stream last night. And I heard your singing."

"H-hey! Komae!"

Distracted, I lost my grip, and Komae slithered away from me and brought his face up close to Shiika's again.

Then he gently put a finger under her chin, lifting it up.

"I seem to have become captivated by your singing voice. How about you and I go sing karaoke after school? I'd like to have the chance to listen to your voice, just you and me, in a quiet, intimate setting...," he whispered sweetly.

"..."

Shiika gazed at him with blank eyes.

She wasn't awestruck, of course. She was half-asleep and looked drowsy.

Komae seemed to be very confident in his approach. He was smirking like he'd won her over already.

"I don't wanna. Sounds like a pain."

"All right. Then, after school, in the classroom, we..."

Realizing that Shiika had just turned him down, he blinked.

"What did you just say?"

"It sounds like a pain. That means a hassle."

"It's...it's not that I don't understand what you said..."

"So then what don't you understand?"

"Um... I mean... Oh, gosh. Ah-ha-ha..."

Komae scratched his cheek, still grinning at Shiika, who tilted her head and observed him.

What happened to the confident playboy from a few seconds ago? He seemed bewildered in the face of Shiika's straightforward rejection. I almost felt a little sorry for the guy.

"What a shock. Usually, the girls all say yes when I sweet-talk them."

"Do they?"

"Well, in over a hundred battles, I guess this is my first defeat."

"Oh," Shiika said, sounding utterly disinterested.

She then said:

"That's odd. You have the voice of a liar."

"...!"

For a moment, Komae's smile disappeared, and he looked shocked.

"Are you saying I'm lying?" he probed.

"Yeah. That voice just now was pitch-black. It's the color of someone hiding something."

"What...? You see sounds as...as colors? Hey, are you serious?"

"Yes."

"How can you decide who's lying and who isn't?"

"I don't know how it works. But when my brother, Gak, lies about something, it's always that color."

I, an innocent bystander, was caught in the crossfire.

Lies and deceptions don't work on Shiika. Having lived under the same roof as her for many years, I knew this was absolutely true without a doubt.

If you tell a lie, she'll catch you immediately. If you want to deceive Shiika, you have to communicate nonverbally or lie by outright omission of information.

With this second talent of hers, she'd be able to play an active role not only as a singer, but as a police officer or a detective.

She'd hate that, though.

"Um... You're..."

"It's Komae. Nokia Komae."

After he said his name, Shiika pointed her finger between his eyes.

"Koma."

For an abbreviation, I think it's a bit too short.

"K-Koma? Well, you can call me whatever you like, but..."

"Koma, you don't seem to be lying with bad intentions. But you ARE hiding something."

Shiika spoke with slow, deliberate intonation.

"..."

Her assertive statement had him closing and opening his mouth.

Then...

"...Pfft! Ha-ha! You really are amusing, Shiika."

He burst into raucous laughter, like a dam breaking.

He bent back and laughed while clutching his stomach.

After laughing for a while, Komae wiped the tears from the corners of his eyes.

"I give! I give! You win. Seriously, I only wanted to tease you a little, but that was some counterattack."

"Right... Peace."

Shiika gave a wilted victory sign in front of Komae. It was as if she'd realized that winning ought to come with some display of rejoicing, only her heart wasn't in it.

"Gah..."

Komae reeled back, as if he'd been shot.

He turned away from Shiika, hiding his slightly flushed face with one hand.

"Darn, this isn't fair... What's happening to me? Getting all excited over something like this... What am I, some geeky middle schooler?"

He was mumbling.

Hmm, could it be that Shiika's cuteness had shot an arrow straight to his heart?

Well, it was hardly surprising. Actually, his appraisal of her up until yesterday, as a drab country girl, was far less fair. He may have awoken to Shiika's charms now, but that didn't mean he was going to get anywhere with her.

"I...I'm off, then. See ya!"

"Byeee."

Shiika waved lazily as Komae walked off. His embarrassment had maxed out, and he'd clearly decided to withdraw.

Completely in control. A villainess who doesn't even know it. My little sister was truly fearsome.

The looks we were getting from all over the classroom seemed to have changed somewhat in nature.

Shiika befuddling Nokia Komae, a top-level student, admired by all... It was clearly something out of the norm.

Surprise, admiration, jealousy. All kinds of emotions were swirling within the classroom.

"..."

But there was one among them...

There was one gaze with a particularly strong emotion behind it.

When I noticed it and looked up, that person hurriedly looked away.

But it was too late. I had seen "her" glaring at Shiika.

Erio Shibuya.

A talent who reigned at the top of this class. Standing above all others with her impressive ability. Or at least, that's the way it should have been.

In actuality, her eyes, while staring at Shiika, were filled with a bitter jealousy.

Her mouth, moving silently.

Not for anyone to hear. Without a doubt, those silent words were for her own rumination.

But just from the movements of her mouth, I could guess what she wanted to say.

Or maybe it just seemed that way to me. After all, I had a pretty twisted personality.

"Who you do think you are, bitch?"

I had the impression she was thinking something along those lines.

…Hmm, perhaps I should treat Erio Shibuya with some extra caution.

If nothing happened, then no harm no foul. But if she tried to mess with Shiika, I would have to make sure to protect her. I couldn't let Shiika get hurt.

It was my duty as her older brother.

◊ ◊ ◊

But despite my misgivings, the morning went by peacefully enough.

Although I felt Erio Shibuya's and the other students' eyes on us, nobody approached, and then it was lunch break.

Like yesterday, lunch was peaceful, with Akiba boasting about her delicious-looking meal.

It was in the afternoon when the problems began.

Today, too, the first class in the afternoon was Vocal Basics. With us all gathered in the studio for vocal lessons on the third floor of the school building, Mr. Afro began his lecture with a triumphant sort of energy.

"All right, gang! Today I'm going to explain that each person's 'vocal range' is different, while we all listen to actual examples of vocalization. Do I have a volunteer?"

Raising his hand jauntily in the air to signal what he was after, Mr. Afro addressed the students with high spirits.

"I will."

Erio Shibuya was the first one to volunteer. Earrings swinging, she got to her feet.

Go, Erio! It had to be you! You're our role model! The students were saying things like that.

"How about one more? I'd like to compare the differences in vocal range between singers, so I'd like at least two people to volunteer."

...There was no response.

The students merely looked at one another. Nobody raised their hand.

(Well, who would want to?)

I thought that as I sat in the corner of the studio with my back against the wall, watching the class unfold.

The teacher was talking about comparing vocal ranges.

It wasn't about physique, bone structure, throat structure, or the individual vocal characteristics of a person, nor was it about trying to determine who was superior.

But to the assembled students, it was all the same thing. To get up in front of the class would mean being compared to Erio Shibuya, a prodigy who, despite being in high school, already had a contract for a major-label debut in the pipes.

Anyone would shrink from being compared to her.

When the teacher called for another volunteer, there were several students who shifted in their seats and looked like they were about to raise their hands. But as soon as they realized they'd be up there with Erio Shibuya, they withdrew and were now silent.

"Hmm. Oh dear, this is a bit of a fix. Well then, I suppose it will just have to be Miss Shibuya and myself doing the demonstration."

"Teacher, can I make a suggestion?"

"Oh. Yes, Miss Shibuya. If you have any good ideas, please feel free to voice them!"

"The girl over there who's sprawled out…"

Erio pointed our way.

"Shiika Ikebukuro. I think it would be good if she sang for us," she said with a grin, as if she was simply being playful.

Shiika, slumped with her back against the wall, twitched.

She looked to me, beside her, and tilted her head curiously.

"She said my name. What for?"

"She wants you to sing in front of everyone. That Erio girl… Maybe she was captivated by your singing like everyone else has been?"

I spoke with heavy sarcasm.

Of course, I knew that wasn't the reason why Erio was doing this.

"If you don't want to, you can say no. I'll get you out of this somehow—"

"Oh, of course she won't mind, will she? When she's such an amazing singer? Please, come and set an example for the class."

Erio spoke loudly, cutting me off as I whispered in Shiika's ear.

The teacher and the students were all gazing at Shiika.

"What do you want to do, Shiika?"

"All I have to do is sing?"

"Apparently."

"Okay. I'll do it, then."

Shrugging and sounding nonchalant, she got to her feet.

Then she walked sluggishly to the front of the classroom, one leg dragging a little.

When Shiika drew level with her, Erio snorted.

"Wow. Thought you'd chicken out."

"Chicken out? Why?"

"Grr."

Erio gnashed her teeth, annoyed by Shiika's display of naivete.

No doubt she'd taken it as Shiika implying that being compared to her was no big deal.

But that wasn't Shiika's intention at all. For Shiika, singing was never a competition. It just came naturally to her, like breathing.

A being possessed of such mental fortitude that she would have no fear in the face of Erio Shibuya... That wasn't Shiika.

To begin with, she had no concept of how skilled and formidable Erio Shibuya was.

Shiika Ikebukuro just didn't see the world like that.

"I said singing, but really, it's just vocalization. Sing '*la*' into this phone. Use whatever register is easiest for you. Then go one octave lower—and one octave higher. This app will determine your vocal range. Isn't technology wonderful? In the old days, we had to vocalize along to a piano and sort of fumble around to find the best vocal range. These days, we have apps to determine it for us."

Mr. Afro whipped out his phone, speaking in enraptured tones.

"All right, Miss Shibuya. Let's start with your natural voice. Your chest voice."

"All right."

Erio nodded and took a deep breath.

Then...

"La-la-la-la-la-la-la-la-la— ♪"

Well, no one was shocked. You couldn't call it singing, just vocalizing, but even that sounded amazing coming from her.

Her wide vocal range, too, was impressive.

When I first noticed Shiika could sing, I was interested in her vocal range and register, and I tried doing some research. Apparently, the vocal range of a standard female is an octave and a half from G3 to C5.

G3 and C5, in other words, goes from the "*so*" we learn in elementary school and junior high music classes to the "*do*," which is two octaves higher. But this kind of terminology is really meant for those obsessed, so feel free to just sort of skim over it.

Women with voices that are higher and lower than average only

differ in the pitch of notes they can produce. If they don't do special training, the range of notes that they can produce will generally fall within this one-and-a-half-octave range.

The wider the range, the richer the variety of songs a person can sing.

Singers with a five-octave singing voice get bragging rights, not only because they can produce high-pitched sounds, but also because they can sing in a wide vocal range.

In that sense, Erio Shibuya's vocal range was truly extraordinary.

A piercing, high-pitched sound rang out across the studio, exceeding what would normally be the limit, yet it retained a beautiful tone.

Voice appraising complete.

Mr. Afro was amazed by the results the app showed.

"Two octaves from F3 to F5 in the natural voice. Six octaves including the whistle register?!"

"Phew... Yep, that's about it."

Shibuya caught her breath and grinned.

"Bravo! Oh, this is something special! I would have liked to compare an alto girl with a soprano girl, but we have seen something unexpectedly amazing today! I can scarcely believe you could go so high in the whistle register—and while maintaining total control, too!"

The teacher applauded.

The notes produced from the whistle register are similar to that of a whistle, and it is higher than falsetto. It's extremely difficult to master, but those who can are able to expand their range of vocal expression. And becoming a top-rated singer, like a genuine high-pitched diva, isn't out of the question if you can produce a whistle voice.

(I mean, yes, it's all very impressive, but haven't we strayed from the subject of the lesson somewhat?)

I sighed inwardly.

Erio Shibuya's abilities were completely beside the point at the moment. Why show off her abilities like this anyhow?

A teacher shouldn't be indulging a student who just wants to show off. What the heck is wrong with this school?

That's our Erio! Only Erio can win! The students were excited, blathering things like that. Shibuya's invisible big old *tengu* nose was no doubt stretching longer and longer, to match her big, swollen head.

"Hmm…"

However, in the hustle and bustle of the studio, only Shiika remained expressionless as she stared at Erio's face.

Erio noticed this as well.

"What? You got a problem?"

"No."

Shiika shook her head. Then…

"I can't express it well, but…something about your voice gives me the ick."

"…Excuse me?!"

At that one comment from Shiika, Erio screeched like a mad wildcat.

Shiika continued unapologetically.

"I noticed it when I heard your I Tried Singing video. There's something weird about you."

"What is your problem? Are you trying to start beef with me?"

"No. It's just a shame that it gives me the ick when you can produce such a wonderful sound."

"…The hell do you know?!"

"Now, now, Miss Shibuya, let's just calm down. And, Miss Ikebukuro, I believe your comments are out of place."

Mr. Afro stepped in, preventing Erio from grabbing Shiika.

The atmosphere was crackling with tension.

In the confusion, Akiba sidled up to me.

"Hey, Gakuto. The way Shiika's talking… Does she by any chance have perfect pitch?"

"It's something beyond that, actually."

"Huh?"

"Shiika sees colors in sounds."

"Really? That's amazing."

Akiba seemed honestly impressed.

But then she suddenly looked suspicious.

"But that doesn't seem to have anything to do with music…"

"That's what you'd think, right…?"

Having said that, I continued.

"Do you know the pitfalls of perfect-pitch education? Oh, it sounds like I'm some know-it-all, but I had to look it up myself."

"Huh. Sounds interesting—let me hear it."

Akiba leaned in.

I began explaining, thinking back to what I'd found out from past research.

"People think absolute pitch is the ability to guess the pitch or melody of a sound just by listening to it or having the ability to reproduce it yourself—"

"I mean, in general terms, that's what it is?"

"No, it's actually more complicated. There are people who are like human tuning forks who, from a single note, can accurately grasp the melody—and recognize the frequency as well."

"Huh."

"So when teaching children to acquire absolute pitch in gifted education programs, it would be quite difficult if they only learned the sound of a specific frequency."

"Specific?"

"For example, a piano that is tuned to start '*la*' at 440 hertz will go up to 466 hertz, 494 hertz, and 523 hertz as you play the ♯ of '*la*,' '*si*,' and '*do*,' in order. Even if you were taught to guess the notes, you might not be able to understand the 480 hertz notes played by pianos with different tunings."

"Ah, I see. So depending on what the premise is, even absolute pitch can change, right?"

"Right. That's why a musician with perfect pitch who was educated at 440 hertz can't match an orchestra that's tuned to 442 hertz. Or if a tuning different from the frequency range that they were educated in becomes popular, well, it's like having a door slammed in their face, see?"

"Aha. So Mana Akihabara is actually a genius musician because she's not constrained by having perfect pitch… Right?"

"I wouldn't go as far as to say genius."

Her take on this was way too self-serving. But whatever.

"Though, you know, Gakuto, what's this explanation have to do with Shiika and her ability?"

"It depends on the conditions, but people can see 7.5 million colors. In other words…"

"The pattern of sounds generated by humans generally falls within this range of colors… Something like that?"

"That's correct."

I was impressed by Akiba's intuition. Not bad for an aspiring composer. Still, I continued.

"Being able to perceive sounds with a much higher degree of accuracy than people who merely possess perfect pitch…THAT is Shiika's big talent."

"Seriously? Wow. Ah, but that's just in terms of listening, right? That doesn't mean she can sing absolutely any sound, right?"

"Well, about that…"

In fact, synesthesia isn't such a rare talent.

In the past, there were wildly varying theories about it occurring in one in one hundred thousand people or one in two thousand people, but according to recent research, about one in every one hundred people has some basic level of synesthesia.

Shiika's synesthesia, however, was a little different from the standard type.

"She can actually SEE the colors."

"?"

Jerking my chin, I urged Akiba to look up front.

Thanks to Mr. Afro's mediation, the situation had calmed down somewhat.

Erio was still glaring at Shiika with an irritated expression, but… perhaps that was to be expected, after having her voice, her biggest source of pride, called into question.

Brotherly favoritism aside, I knew that Shiika wasn't the type of person to hurt someone else for no reason. There must have been a good reason for her to have said Erio's singing gave her "the ick," but Erio had no way of knowing that.

"Th-then, let's have Miss Ikebukuro try it next."

"...Okay."

Mr. Afro was awkwardly trying to move the class along. Shiika nodded, her head moving only slightly.

She took a step forward.

Phoo... She took just one small breath.

Then...

All of a sudden, the entire atmosphere changed.

It was like watching a picture being painted before your very eyes.

Like being tossed atop a hill that has a rainbow.

"La-la-la." That was all she was singing.

There shouldn't have been any artistry to speak of.

But the sounds Shiika emitted were so beautiful, so precise... It was as if Shiika Ikebukuro was no longer human, but a musical instrument.

Akiba, Mr. Afro, Nokia Komae, the other students, and I...

Even Erio Shibuya, who by rights should have been angry.

We were all fascinated by what was happening, as if our souls were being tugged from our bodies.

"All done."

"...! Y-yes! Ah... Thank you very much..."

Hearing Shiika proclaim that she was finished seemed to snap Mr. Afro out of a daze.

Then, looking at his phone screen...

"Well, Miss Ikebukuro's vocal range is from G3 to E5. It's a common range for a woman, including natural voice and falsetto."

"...Hmph. And after you acted so arrogant, too."

Erio snorted.

"Normal voice. You think you can get to the top with that?"

"No."

Shiika shook her head.

"I'm not really interested in the top."

"What...?"

"But never mind that. How was my voice?"

"...!"

Shiika brought her face close to Erio's, and Erio leaned back.

"I chose only beautiful colors. How did it sound to you?" Shiika said, her golden eyes on Erio.

"What do you mean...?"

Hesitating, Erio bit her lip. Then...

"Who freakin' cares?!"

She pushed Shiika aside and ran out of the studio.

Everyone looked stunned.

Then the class began to break out in chatter.

Some people condemned Shiika's words and deeds. Others muttered honest impressions about Shiika's voice being beautiful. While some said that Erio's six-octave range was special—and that Shiika was only mediocre.

"...They don't get it."

I whispered in a voice that only Akiba beside me could hear.

Akiba pounced on that immediately.

"What don't they get?"

"Having a wide vocal range is just one way for a singer to distinguish themselves, that's all. In the business, many songs are written for women with standard voices to sing. As a singer, that's basically all you need."

Of course, having a wide vocal range is no drawback. However, it's possible to have a very expressive voice without one.

Just as Shiika had demonstrated.

"Indeed. Regardless of the vocal range, Shiika's voice was quite lovely just then."

"I know. Using her voice like an instrument, manipulating it freely. It's not just her synesthesia. It's her vocals that make Shiika a prodigious talent."

The source of all the controversy herself was staring at the doorway of the studio, the one Erio had just left through. She ignored the gazes directed her way.

Even though I was Shiika's brother, I was just a normal person. I had no way of knowing what thoughts were truly swirling within her mind.

Chapter 3:
A Collaboration

Despite a lingering element of anxiety about how things stood with Erio Shibuya since that one class, time had been ticking by peacefully since, with no real incidents of note.

The average number of views we were getting on Impachi Live was five thousand, and the occasional popular song even managed to reach ten thousand views. So I was confident we'd be able to earn a sum worth feeling good about.

Then the last day of April rolled around.

"*La-la-la.* ♪ Oh, what a wonderful morning. Oh, how I've been waiting for this day~ ♪"

I was in a good mood.

I pirouetted around our place, skillfully avoiding the mess on the floor, brandishing my phone in one hand.

Incidentally, I used an operatic intonation with my little song just then. Oh yes, I was in high spirits indeed!

"Gak... Can you keep it down?"

"Ah, Shiika! You've finally woken up."

"I was sleeping. You were so noisy, you woke me up."

Shiika emerged from her room, rubbing her eyes.

She wore a baggy T-shirt that covered her thighs. Languidly, she made her way to the kitchen.

"Milk, milk...," she muttered, and scratched at the refrigerator like a pet begging to be fed.

"Yes, yes, I'll get your milk," I said, heading to the refrigerator and pulling out a carton, pouring the white liquid into a glass.

Shiika brought the cup to her lips and drank, making loud gulping sounds.

Milk dripped from the edges of her mouth.

"Ah, stop! You're such a messy drinker! Oh, look, you've soiled your shirt again. Now I have to wash that! It's a big hassle, don't you realize?"

"Eh?"

"I wasn't talking to you! Don't force yourself to converse on my behalf!"

I wiped her off with a towel.

Why was it up to me to babysit her like this—and right from the moment she woke up? How frustrating.

But today I supposed it didn't really matter. I'd just give the shirt a quick rinse.

That milk's gonna stink if you don't wash it properly, you say? Ah yes. But you've got to laugh, haven't you? On a day like today.

After all, today was the first day we'd be getting our living expenses after entering this school!

"Rejoice, Shiika."

"Hmm?"

"The result of your efforts will now be revealed. Tuna—or maybe even steak!"

"Wow..."

One million yen or two million yen? Just from looking at the earnings of popular WayTubers and streamers, I estimated at least that amount.

"Now, let us go! To enjoy our Golden Experience!"

My chest swelling with lofty thoughts of pure gold and riches, I accessed the account balance page on my phone.

The amount deposited from Ryouran High School Inc. was...?!

* * *

43,500 yen.

"...Huh?"

Isn't that too little? That couldn't be right. That was far too low to be the real amount.

Sure, earning this much money as a regular high schooler would be difficult. At an hourly part-time wage of one thousand yen, I'd have to work for forty-five hours to earn that.

But this... This just didn't make sense!

This is a spectacular school, attended by young people aiming to enter the entertainment world! The students at the top should be earning over a hundred million yen per month! Even the average student should be able to earn over five hundred thousand yen! I was hoping for that level of economic prosperity.

This amount... It'd be swallowed up instantly by the rent and grocery budget...

"Can we get tuna sushi with this?"

"Sorry, but the best we can get with this is bean sprouts. Maybe we could add some sesame oil on top, as a special luxury."

"Oh no... After I tried my best and all..."

Shiika was shocked and looked despondent.

I felt the same way.

We dolled her up with makeup, had her sing popular songs with her amazing voice... What more did these people want?

◊ ◊ ◊

"It has to be a collaboration, doesn't it?"

Before morning classes had begun, I whined about our paltry payment situation to our trusty pal, Mana Akihabara, and that was the first thing she said in response.

"She's good-looking, and she's talented. Since you have those two things, all you need to do is increase her chances of gaining exposure. And the quickest method would be to collab with the popular streamers."

"Oh, but of course!"

Akiba always came through with the goods. Ah yes, she was the best at helping me pull myself up by the bootstraps.

"...You're thinking something rude about me right now, aren't you?"

"No, you fool! I'm thinking respectful thoughts! I was thinking how great a person you are to have in our corner!"

"Oh, you've done it now. Now I'm pissed. I'm not going to give you ANY suggestions for collabs now."

"Argh! I'm sorry! Please forgive me, Mistress Akiba, Queen Mana! Please have mercy!"

"Oh, all right then. If you're willing to kowtow before me to that extent...then I guess I'm honor bound to share with you my great wisdom," Akiba said in a magnanimous tone.

Gazing at her smug face, a sudden question came to mind.

"Well, you seem comfortable, Akiba. You get about the same number of views as Shiika, but you're doing all right for yourself money-wise, aren't you?"

"Our base pay is the same, but there's also my income from tips to factor in."

"Tips?! You get tips for just doing roundups of other people's comments?!"

"When people tip to have their comments seen, they earn the right to ask certain favors of me. Like taking photos of their favorite students in class and doing collaborations, that sort of thing."

"Wow. You're an industrious girl, eh."

"Another backhanded compliment from you? Oh, whatever. It's not like I'm breaking any rules now, is it?"

"I thought voyeurism WAS against the rules."

"Wrong. According to the school rules, it's perfectly allowed for students, staff, etcetera, to take general snapshots inside school grounds."

"Are you serious?"

"Forbidding it would only inconvenience everyone. Lots of people record dance and singing lessons for later reference. And filming movies and taking artsy photographs is part of the curriculum. Ah, what a convenient loophole it is…for me. *Tra-la-la.* ♪"

"Always sniffing around for loopholes, I bet."

Maybe she WOULD end up being some kind of big shot in the future.

"Shiika's content is taking the easy path. If you're gonna make actual money in that field, you're gonna need your views to be ten to a hundred times what they are now."

"That amount is totally unrealistic… How many students have actually achieved results like that?"

"In our department, only Erio Shibuya, I'd say. You remember when her first stream got three hundred thousand views in record time?"

"Ah yes, that was amazing."

"Go and look at her past streams archive. You won't believe your eyes."

"All right, all right, I'm checking it… What the heck is this?!"

Accessing Erio Shibuya's channel for the first time in a while, I was astonished by what I found.

Her most viewed stream had the following figures:

[Views] 4,583,360 [Likes] 43,284 [Revenue] 1,052,500 yen

Those were some large figures… But she had other streams that were doing just as well. There were even a few more that had over a million views. Her average view count was around seven hundred thousand. And she had over half a million subscribers.

"These numbers are ridiculous. It's like they were randomly given by an elementary schooler who doesn't have any concept of numbers. This is just too amazing to be true."

"Well, with figures like those, just imagine how much income she's getting paid by the academy."

"Guh! Oh, I'm so jealous!"

"You don't have time to be jealous. Think. Here's an account that

earns big money. This could be our chance to increase our own numbers, you know?"

"...! Of course! For an effective collaboration, it's got to be..."

"Indeed. In the Music Department, there is no better option. Erio
Shibuya is at the top!"

"I see, I see...! Oh no, darn it!"

My hope turned into despair.

After her altercation with Shiika in class, I couldn't see Erio Shibuya
agreeing to one.

It was finished...done for... The collaboration strategy...

"Isn't it about time you went and apologized to Erio? Maybe she'll
forgive you if you get down on your knees and lick her shoes?"

"That's disgusting. I'd rather die."

But she was right.

"Darn it, what the heck am I supposed to do?!"

I writhed around, clutching my hair.

Shiika, the key to all of this, was snoozing peacefully at her desk,
totally oblivious to the gravity of the situation.

Well, solving the nitty-gritty issues is my job. All Shiika had to do
was show off her talent.

Now then, what to do...? I racked my brain.

Then I felt someone's gaze.

It wasn't a mere glance. The individual was gazing at Shiika,
impassioned.

"Hmm...?"

Looking toward them, I saw a student who quickly averted his eyes.

It was our redheaded classmate, Nokia Komae.

His hair was short, so I was able to see that his ears had gone slightly
pink.

Come to think of it, ever since the Vocal Basics class when Shiika
and Erio had their spat, Nokia had been paying more attention to us
than before.

"Hey, Akiba. What about him?"

"So you noticed him, too, huh, Gakuto?"

Akiba was grinning like a child with a brand-new toy.

Matching her smile, I smirked, too.

"Just out of interest…what are HIS numbers like?"

"Pretty high, actually. Not quite at Erio Shibuya's level, but his stream archive gets an easy three hundred thousand views, and his songs are used in tons of other vids as BGM. He's also well-known for being a major songwriter for Erio."

"I see… Mwah-ha-ha! I see it! A light on the horizon!"

"You mean, the strategy?"

"Yes. I see our next move clearly now. And that move is…"

Both Akiba and I were on the same page.

We spoke simultaneously.

""Attack her Achilles' heel!""

Once that decision was made, action was swift.

I moseyed over to Nokia and flung my arm around his shoulders.

"Komae, my friend! ♪"

"Agh. Wh-what do you want, Gakuto? Don't approach me acting all creepy like that."

"Oh, I didn't mean to creep you out. I've just been wanting to get closer to you, is all…"

"Huh? Get closer? You've never once given me that impression since school started. This is all highly suspicious, you know!"

"You've fallen head over heels for Shiika, haven't you?"

"Say WHAT?"

Excellent, he confirmed it. Thanks for that. The most easily read-able reaction in the world.

"And that being the case, shouldn't you try to get along with her elder brother, in other words, me?"

"D-don't go speaking for me. I don't particularly have a crush on Shi…"

"Oh, so that's the attitude you're going to take?"

"Wh-what do you mean?"

"I'm looking for a collaborator right now. I'm searching for a com-poser who can provide music."

"Wh-what?"

"Well, what a shame. I guess I have no choice but to go with some totally unknown, handsome vocaloid producer instead...," I whispered suggestively...right into his ear.

Then Nokia's face turned pale.

"Wait, wait, wait! I'll do it! I'll collaborate with you! Please let me compose a song for Shiika!"

He bit.

Hook, line, sinker—heck, the whole fishing rod.

"Heh-heh-heh. Then you should have just agreed like a good boy in the beginning. Men playing hard to get is just, like, not a thing."

"No, no, some girls love it. That whole hot-and-cold guy thing."

Quiet now, Akiba.

...I apologize, though, for speaking as if I had any idea about women's preferences.

But returning to the point...

"If you're going to do it, then hop to it. Compose a suitable tune for Shiika at once."

"I will! Just leave it to me, brother!"

"Don't get carried away. You don't have permission to call me brother."

"It...it was just a joke, Gakuto. Please, there's no need to get so angry."

"Well, when I'm dealing with a player like yourself, I have to be on my guard... So how many days does it take to make a song?"

"If I had two weeks..."

"Oh, deary me! My thumb is about to slip and send a message to another male composer!"

"One week! One week, then..."

"*Hello. My name is Gakuto Ikebukuro. I am in need of a composer for a project, and...*"

"Three days! I'll have it done in three days!"

"Oh, all right. That should be adequate."

The feeling it gave me, negotiating favorably with a high-ranking opponent, someone who boasted an overwhelming number of views... Oh, it was delectable.

A man with a crush is a weak being indeed.

As a handsome playboy, he ought to have had a lot of experience with girls. His naive, starry-eyed reaction had surprised me. Perhaps Shiika really was just too charming? Ah yes, I would expect no less of my own sister.

"By the way, what are you planning to have me do during the stream with Shiika? Pass the Pocky from mouth to mouth? A game of Twister?"

"Huh? Hey! Get your mind out of the gutter when it comes to my sister!"

"No, no, no, you've got it wrong! I apologize! I took it too far!"

"Just write a song and sing it. If you two suddenly start acting all pally during the stream, it won't be convincing."

Akiba nodded, agreeing with me.

Narrowing my eyes even more devilishly, I continued.

"A sense of reserve and decorum is essential when a man and woman collaborate on a project. Komae, you and your torrid love affairs... They're gonna bring trouble, you know?"

"Ugh... It's so true that I can't even say anything in my defense..."

"It's all in the timing. After you've provided a few songs for Shiika, the fans, too, will gradually begin to accept your partnership. Let's make a real go of this, okay?"

"Gakuto...! You're...a fine fellow!"

Deeply moved, Nokia burst into tears and gripped my hand.

Well, Shiika had no interest in dating anyway, so it would be very easy for me to make sure that Nokia's love went unrequited. Still, I decided to keep that inconvenient truth safely stored within me.

At any rate, it looked like we had a standing agreement for Nokia to write songs for us.

A collaboration with someone boasting far superior figures to

Shiika's. This would boost our numbers into the stratosphere, no doubt about it.

But then I paused. There was one thing, just one thing that bothered me.

"Come to think of it, is it okay to provide songs for Shiika, from a contractual point of view?"

"Huh? Contractual?"

"I mean, you're also writing songs for Erio, right? I heard you two were, like, a duo. It's not like an exclusive contract, is it?"

"Oh no, not at all."

When I dropped my voice to a conspiratorial whisper, Nokia brushed aside my concerns.

"Erio's the only one who has a contract with the record label. I'm a totally replaceable cog."

"Huh, I see, so that's how it is."

"I actually wrote her debut song. But as far as the label is concerned, they want to make her the next massive diva, and no doubt they're going to pull out all the stops. I heard they've already got a super-popular composer all lined up for her."

Nokia spoke with sarcasm.

His tone was lighthearted, but it sounded like he was jealous, resigned, and all other sorts of negative emotions.

It was a little surprising.

Nokia Komae was one of the most influential and popular students in this classroom. But even he felt like there was a kind of impenetrable wall between him and his higher-ranked opponent. He seemed like he had it all yet look at him now... Looking so unfulfilled.

"Well anyway, you don't have to worry about contracts—or about me not bringing my A game. I plan to write the best possible song I can for Shiika."

Nokia flexed his biceps and gave a dazzling smile. His arms were slender but toned. A surprising hint of muscle. Even his body was the kind that girls like. Darn him. I felt slightly jealous.

"Great! Counting on you!" I responded.

Even though there's no way I'm ever going to consider you as a boyfriend candidate for Shiika!

◊ ◊ ◊

Three days passed since then.

Today was Saturday.

A day known to be part of the weekend.

My take on it had changed a little since entering Ryouran High, but it still felt weird to think of Saturday as being the weekend.

For a shut-in, every day was the weekend and every day was the weekday. There was no difference among them. So it was hard to wrap my head around it after living like that.

Since my online friends were working adults, you might think I'd be able to figure that out when they're online. But when you've got your days and nights reversed, you can't do that, either. Even working adults log on only after they get home, and people rarely discuss their job online, so I never really gave it much thought.

But today... Today is part of a wonderful weekend, which means no school! That's how I've been feeling these days. Weekends are so good, if they were a substance, they'd be addictive.

"And there's even a maid to take care of everything around me. Is this heaven?"

"Who are you calling a maid? I'll knock you out!"

The female friend in the cotton gloves and mask, putting our household garbage into a garbage bag...in other words, Akiba, gave me a glare and a few choice words.

"Well, an angel, then. Choose the one you like best!"

"I don't want to be called either! I'm not doing this for fun, you know!"

She heaved a sigh, looking annoyed.

"Gakuto, why don't you clean before you invite someone over to your house?"

"Eh, it's too much of a hassle."

"Then don't have visitors! How can you bear having someone else enter this...this pigsty?"

"Well, I have to invite people over. Today's the day that Komae is going to deliver his song. We need to listen to it and have a strategy meeting to determine the best way to debut it."

"Why are you saying 'we' like it's a foregone conclusion that I'll help?"

"Well, we're friends. Working together to complete missions is what friends do, right?"

"Hmm, maybe in online games. But this is reality…"

"Don't be so nitpicky. Ryouran High's system is like a game, after all."

"Hmm, you may have a… No, no, I disagree! Your reasoning is totally ridiculous!"

Akiba shook her head, as if to show she couldn't be persuaded. Tsk, she's so stubborn.

"Actually, I need your help in particular, Akiba."

"What for? With Shiika's singing ability, it should be easy enough to judge whether the song's any good, right?"

"No, no, that's not the case at all."

Actually, Shiika and I can tell a good song from a bad one.

Akiba doesn't know it, but Shiika was a pretty popular WayTube Vsinger. As Seeker's manager, I listened to a lot of songs and gained a good grasp of what genres of music show off Shiika's voice the best.

But the knowledge I'd gained from that didn't necessarily apply to Impachi Live.

After entering the academy, I'd learned that through bitter experience.

"I need to know if the song will get toes tapping… If it'll make a splash on Impachi Live. You're the one who does informative videos on the service, right? With you around, we'll have a much better chance of success than if it was just Shiika and me trying to put our heads together."

"Well, you're not wrong there."

"Leave it to the pros, that's what I say! Right, partner?"

"…Tsk. You're certainly presumptuous."

Sighing, Akiba tied the bursting garbage bag nice and tight.

Throwing it against the wall, she gave a cynical smile.

"Still, maybe that's where your talent lies, Gakuto."

"MY talent, you say?"

"Yeah. The ability to get other people to do stuff for you."

"Oh, hey, that makes me sound cool. No one's ever said I had a talent before."

"In other words, you piggyback off others."

"Hey, now it sounds less cool!"

"In the future, I bet you're going to end up some rich woman's boy toy."

"You really think so? Gosh, that sounds amazing."

"You call that amazing? You really are trash, aren't you?"

As she spoke, Akiba began scrubbing the carpet around our low table with carpet cleaner that she'd brought from home.

...Actually, at this present moment, Akiba was the one doing the most for me. Did that make me her boy toy? I decided not to mention it.

Still, she came when I summoned her and even helped clean, claiming she couldn't stand a messy place. She was made of the right stuff. As for what that stuff was, exactly... Well, I decided not to overthink it.

"But I'm in no position to mock others, I guess. After all, I'm here with ulterior motives of my own."

"Oh, good. That's a lot better for my conscience."

"Oh, you've got a conscience, then? Well, you and your issues aside, I figured if I forge a strong connection with Shiika, it'll pay off in the future."

"So you've come to appreciate Shiika's great talent."

"When I saw her going up against Erio, I got the chills. It was like a goddess descending from the heavens. I realized she's no small fry after all."

"Is that like when the god of creation blesses you?"

After all that talk about not being able to create anything without the god of creation's intervention.

While the two of us bantered back and forth...

Brrrr. I heard my phone vibrating on the low table.

"That's him!"

Cutting off our conversation, I snatched up my phone.

I'd gotten a message from Komae.

"HOW ABOUT THIS?" And that was all… Until I saw there was an audio file attached.

"It's here! It's ready! Shiika! It's your new song!"

"Wha—?"

I slammed my hand down on the table, and Shiika emerged from beneath it like a hermit crab.

You may be wondering what she was doing under there. Well, Shiika likes dark, enclosed spaces. No need to be concerned about it.

"New song… From Koma?"

"Yes, yes, from Komae!"

"Wanna listen."

She turned her head toward me.

I grabbed the headphones I'd set out and put them on Shiika's head. Then I connected them to my phone. I transferred the file to Shiika's and Akiba's phones, too. Then I pressed PLAY.

The most important thing to consider was if this song fit Shiika's vibe.

If it overcame that first hurdle, Akiba and I would then begin our appraisals.

Everyone closed their eyes and listened to the song.

The music file was titled "Study, Party, Candy" …It was…

"Huh?"

I mumbled aloud, surprising myself.

When I glanced at Akiba, she seemed to be a little surprised, too. Perhaps she'd had the same impression.

In short, it was an upbeat song.

It was already apparent from the title. It was a fun, poppy melody that would no doubt raise the roof if, for example, a group of friends sang it at karaoke. Putting aside the question of whether urban legends like friends who go to karaoke together actually exist…it was definitely that kind of vibe.

It was a good song. A song that made you want to dance. A fun song.

But I guess that was my main issue with it.

In the classroom, Shiika Ikebukuro was languid, a habitual desk snoozer—and known to march to the beat of her own drum and daydream... I mean, you get the picture.

Actually, Shiika was the kind of girl to lurk in a dark shadow in the corner. Even during her Seeker performances, she usually sang songs with a sort of cool, reserved outlook.

"This is the kind of song he wrote for Shiika? What is he trying to play at?"

"Yeah, but it's pretty good."

Akiba immediately objected to my criticisms.

"This song could blow up."

"Really?"

"Yeah, the Dance Department students will be hooked on a song like this. It's practically screaming for choreography. If you play your cards right, this song could blow up on Impachi Live and have a ripple effect."

"A ripple effect... You mean, like attract the attention of actual celebrities and famous performers?"

"No, you dolt. I mean, that would be sweet, but that's not what I meant."

Akiba gathered herself, then continued.

"I'm talking about ordinary users."

"Ordinary?"

"That's right. Normal high school girls or female college students. Not even students of Ryouran High, just the general public."

"Impachi Live has that much influence?"

"Yeah. Actually, it usually goes that way when someone really blows up on Impachi Live. If you can get the general public talking about you, that would be the best possible outcome."

According to Akiba, that was the biggest difference between Way-Tube and Impachi Live.

The latter was more of a small online community, with streamers having a core fan base. Apparently, there were as many streamers and uploaders as there were viewers.

In the past, WayTube was also a platform made up of amateurs, but with the way the service took off—drawing the attention of large companies—the number of viewers was now skewed to only a few popular channels with strong influence. There was no longer a system in place where videos from amateur creators can take off and go viral.

With that said, Akiba gave Shiika a sideways glance.

"Still, it all depends on Shiika."

"Yeah. No matter how good the song is, if Shiika can't step up to the plate, it'll all be pointless."

Akiba and I looked at Shiika.

She was listening attentively as the song entered its second verse.

"Hmm, hmm, hmm…"

Then she let out a strange, slow humming sound.

Rolling the melody around her tongue. Like she was tuning her own instrument.

After a while, Shiika nodded emphatically.

She opened her eyes.

"It's good. I like this song."

"Really?!"

"Yeah… Hey, Gak. What kind of songs has Koma composed until now?"

"Komae's songs? Er, I don't know, honestly. I know he writes songs for Erio, and… Um…"

I started looking it up on my phone.

In addition to her Impachi Live account, Erio also had a WayTube channel, where she'd uploaded samples of all the songs she'd released so far. All of them were composed by NOKIA (Nokia Komae's stage name).

I checked the first few seconds of each of her songs. I also got a good look at her thumbnails.

There were multiple different genres of music. But despite the variety, I saw a common theme emerging.

"It's kinda like…like she sings a lot of difficult songs."

Songs that showcased Erio's impressive vocal range. Songs that demanded impressive singing techniques.

To be blunt... It was as if she was trying to bludgeon her listeners over the head with her own talent.

Of course, that wasn't a bad thing, per se.

Dictators tend to attract the masses, after all.

Her overbearing talent did seem to lend her a certain air of charisma, capable of charming large numbers of fans. In fact, I could think of no better songs than these for the artist known as Erio Shibuya.

"I thought so."

Shiika seemed to grasp my naive impression and agreed with it.

"Up until now, Koma has been limited to certain types of sounds. So..."

So he wrote that kind of song. This song, especially for Shiika.

"He wants to make music more like this. This song... It's imbued with that strong sentiment."

"So it's a new challenge for Komae, too."

"Perhaps."

A song for someone new, someone he hadn't been partnering with ever since junior high. Written by someone with great talent, trying to break out of his shell, and offered to Shiika, with the utmost reverence and respect.

"With this song, I think... I think I can see a new sort of sketch emerging."

"Then we have to record it."

After all, that was the reason why Shiika continued with her online singing activities.

Shiika sees colors in sound.

And in songs, she sees images.

In order to enter amazing worlds she's never seen, Shiika encloses herself in dark rooms, quietly weaving sounds like dreams.

I thought it would be a long, long journey until Shiika encountered an entirely new sort of image.

And by returning to the classroom, a place I'd hoped to never see again... It had only been a month or so of school, and I could scarcely believe that Shiika had encountered a new image this fast.

The world works in mysterious ways.

After that...

We spent an entire half day recording Shiika's song, and—with Akiba's direction—we decided how we were going to release and stream it.

Ryouran High's Shiika Ikebukuro, with her first original song, "Study, Party, Candy."

That fated song, perfectly launched, and featured on Akiba's regular streaming roundup video.

[Views] 1,206,990 [Likes] 50,111 [Revenue] 285,000 yen

Shiika Ikebukuro bagged her first video with a million views. And her subscribers reached the ten thousand benchmark.

It wasn't quite at the level of Erio Shibuya's numbers, but for a female student who'd been disparaged as a local karaoke singer, they were unbelievable.

In class, Shiika was suddenly the center of attention.

For better or for worse.

Chapter 4:
A Confrontation

The school gate had become a defined boundary line. I could feel it on my skin, how the way people were looking at Shiika had changed, and how many more were staring at her. No one had looked our way as we walked from the station to school, but as soon as we crossed the threshold of the school gates, we were the object of everyone's attention, as if Shiika was a celebrity.

The general public wasn't aware of her, of course, but she was well-known within the small community of Ryouran High. That much was evident.

I never wanted Shiika to stand out that much. But she needed to get good scores if we wanted to eat, so there was nothing I could do but accept it.

I sighed, defeated.

"So this is how the world looks after you get a million views. How does it feel, Miss Famous?"

"Guh... Grrr..."

Shiika, the Miss Famous in question, was suddenly shy again in a way she hadn't been for a while. She was cowering behind me, growling softly like a dog on high alert.

Her long bangs flopped over her eyes, covering them. It was her way of asserting her will, of refusing to let the public see her completely.

"And it seems there have been rumors circulating that you're actually an extrovert. Don't be shocked if people come over wanting to talk to you, okay?"

Shiika sang the "Study, Party, Candy" song that Komae had written, and she had done it with great gusto while wearing makeup. Quite a few people in the comments section seemed to be under the mistaken impression that this performance reflected her true personality.

For a while now, a few students had been shooting furtive glances at her, as if they were deciding whether to come and talk to her. I expected a surprise attack at any moment.

"Stay away... Just stay back..."

Peeking through her long bangs, Shiika was trying to curse them, like she was some sort of vengeful spirit.

"It might be quicker to just get used to it, you know?"

"Impossible..."

Shiika shook her head furiously, her long hair becoming more disheveled. I felt her press herself even harder against my back.

This was serious.

She'd been relatively okay ever since we entered the academy, since nobody really paid either of us much attention. Also, she'd been excited by the school's variety of sounds and colors.

Even during her confrontation with Erio Shibuya in the studio, Shiika had been able to ignore the gazes of the other students because she was so focused on music.

She didn't want to be the center of attention when there was nothing else going on. That was the antithesis of everything Shiika Ikebukuro.

Still, whether Shiika wanted it or not, showing her skills meant garnering attention. Clout comes with its own limitations. As long as we had something we wanted to gain from this, Shiika would just have to acclimate.

Since Shiika was terrible at this sort of thing, this was where I came in.

All I could do, at times like this, was act as a sort of human shield for Shiika.

"I need a wall, Gak. Please... Grrr..."

"All right, all right. I'll do what I can, Princess."

As her elder brother, I will protect my sister from all kinds of trouble. Bring it on.

But my determination shattered the moment we entered the classroom.

I had a bad feeling when I heard voices arguing loudly from the hallway, and after opening the door, those feelings were confirmed.

"Say it! Why did you team up with her, you traitor?!"

"I'm free to compose songs for anyone!"

In the classroom, Erio Shibuya and Nokia Komae were arguing.

Erio had grabbed Komae by the scruff of his shirt. He was backed up against the wall so he couldn't escape. The look she was giving him was terrifying.

There was no one helping her in her attack on Komae. The other students were just standing around, stunned by the fight that was taking place in front of them.

"But why does it have to be HER? You saw the way she insulted me!"

"What do I care about that? I made a song for a good singer, and that's it!"

"You... Are you being serious right now? How dare you. If it wasn't for you, I'd..."

But Erio stopped midsentence. Then she noticed that Shiika and I had entered the classroom. She glowered at us.

I braced myself for some kind of curse. Her eyes were full of hatred, but she said nothing and returned her gaze to Komae.

"So you're severing ties with me, is that it?"

"Huh? No, I never said that. Why would I do that?"

"Isn't that exactly what you're saying, though?!"

"Hey, hey, I'm begging you, calm down. You're a talented artist, lauded by everyone, so why are you freaking out?"

"Tch... Oh, just shut up...!"

Snarling, Erio pushed Komae away, then fled from the classroom at a run.

"Erio! Wait!"

He raised his hand, but Komae's shoulders sagged, and he sighed. Then, awkwardly scratching his cheek, he apologized to the others, his cheeky playboy grin returning. "Sorry for all the commotion, guys."

Shiika and I sat down next to Akiba, who'd already been seated.

Akiba, who had seen everything, leaned in to speak to us. She was frowning.

"It's too early in the morning for such an ugly display, don'cha think?"

"You said it."

"Jealousy is an ugly thing, isn't it? When Erio Shibuya saw that someone else got a million views on a stream, she completely blew her top."

"She's jealous of Shiika's view count? I thought she was jealous about her poaching Komae?"

I had to ask. It hadn't occurred to me that Erio would be jealous of Shiika.

Akiba nodded.

"If she had a crush on Komae, all his flirting with the other girls would have made her snap. So it's not that. It's Shiika's view count. It's too good, and she can't take it."

"Huh. But Erio could get a million views as easy as blinking."

"She's recognized the impact of this new song. Its significance is obvious—to Erio Shibuya as well."

"What is the significance?"

"That the one million views you got is a million views you wouldn't have if you hadn't gotten lucky."

As she spoke, Akiba showed me her phone. She had the Impachi Live app open.

A lot of users had been posting and streaming videos using the hashtag #StudyPartyCandy.

There were a lot of girls dancing to the music, performing choreography that didn't exist in the first place. Akiba pointed to one of the thumbnails.

"See this one? The top student of Ryouran High's Dance Department. Her name's Ootsuka. But she goes by the stage name Ryuzetsuran."

"Oh, you mentioned this student before, didn't you?"

"Yeah. She's a hip-hop dancer, but even within hip-hop, it's pretty liberal, or rather, it's like she's trying to incorporate more and more outside cultures into her style. Apparently, she's taken a liking to this song, and it's gotten popular within the Dance Department."

"Huh. So in a sense, it's thanks to Ootsuka that we've got a million views."

"Right. In one go, both the song and Shiika have gained fame. Within the school, at least."

That pompous phrasing seemed to hit the nail on the head.

I voiced a hypothesis that had crossed my mind.

"So you're saying that it hasn't spread to the general users of Impachi Live yet... Right?"

"Correct. If it spread that far, ten million views wouldn't have been out of the question. But even though it's blown up, it's still only known by the people inside and around Ryouran High."

"A million views seemed so exciting, but I guess it wasn't an absolute victory after all..."

"But think of it this way. A stroke of luck got you to one million. Now Erio Shibuya's running scared. If you keep this up, Shiika could even steal the top spot from her."

"Ride the wave, huh... Still, being the object of jealousy isn't a great prospect."

I didn't want anyone out there gunning for my sister. This situation seemed fraught with danger.

I glanced over at my little sister beside me, wondering if Shiika was okay.

"..."

She was silently staring at the classroom door.

She looked a little different now, compared to the extreme shyness she'd shown earlier. She was no longer showing fear in response to all the stares she was getting. Instead, she appeared to be deep in thought, concentrating on something.

"Are you okay?"

When I checked in with her, Shiika nodded.

"Yeah. I'm fine."

"Hmm, it doesn't seem like you're fine?"

"Yeah."

She didn't deny it.

"That girl… It was Eri Shibuya, wasn't it?"

"It's Erio. But, eh, I guess it doesn't matter."

"Right. The girl called Eri. That voice she showed just now… It was the prettiest of all."

"What…? When she was yelling before?"

"Yes. When she was berating Koma. That voice. It was more of a natural hue than the other times she sang."

"Huh. What was natural about her ranting voice, then?"

"The rant wasn't the important part…"

"All right, let's begin homeroom. I have important news today, so listen carefully."

Just as Shiika was about to explain what she meant, the teacher entered the classroom.

Cut off midconversation. Oh well. I gave up on chatting and looked toward the front.

The female homeroom teacher, who had dark circles under her eyes and looked exhausted, wrote *Midterm Examination* on the blackboard and put her hands down on the teacher's desk. Ignoring the fact that Erio wasn't present, she started talking.

"As announced on the school's portal site, there will be a midterm exam in two weeks. It's fairly laid-back compared to something like a regular high school's midterm exam, so there's no need to fret too much. Have a look at the site for more details. Dismissed."

The homeroom teacher's explanation was over. There seemed to be no other information available apart from what was written on the website.

I guess it didn't matter that not every student was present and accounted for at their desks.

(Still, this is kinda…)

Just when we'd finally started getting good numbers, and I could actually hope for some high scores, I had to walk into a classroom argument, and now this… Midterm exams?

(School life is…a lot to handle.)

I couldn't help but sigh.

◊ ◊ ◊

"This is bad."

Right after homeroom, we were heading to our next class. That was when Akiba started muttering, biting her thumbnail.

Our first period today was a Hip-hop Music class. It was being held in a dedicated classroom located in the basement of the building where the studios and other facilities were located.

A lot of the students seemed to be in high spirits, looking forward to the class, but Akiba didn't seem so happy.

Shiika, who was watching the situation, held out a small zip-up bag.

"Here, have some gummies. Full of magnesium."

"Whoa. Yikes. I didn't peg you as the type to show concern for others, Shiika."

"Fulfilling obligations."

"Oh, right. Yes, I helped you. So I guess now you're in my debt. Ah, okay, that's a relief."

Did she think Shiika was some sort of demon?

Shiika's not of this world, maybe, and you can never tell what's going on in her mind, but she's capable of showing concern for others. It's just very subtle. Very, very subtle. Like, blink and you'll miss it.

"I doubt I'm low on magnesium or anything… But thanks, I'll take some."

"Yeah."

"Nom. Oh, hey… These are pretty good."

Akiba took the bag of gummies from Shiika and popped one into her mouth.

"So what's bad?"

"The midterm exam."

"Oh, that's all? Well, the teacher said it's more laid-back than a regular high school's exams, right? No problem."

"You blissful fool… You haven't seen the site, have you?"

"I can just check it later."

"You'd better check it now. Or the future might be dark for you."

"You don't have to be so dramatic. Okay, let's see…"

I took out my phone and accessed the portal site.

I tapped on ABOUT THE MIDTERM EXAMINATION and scanned the rules.

About the Midterm Examination

1. **Our school does not conduct midterm examinations for each class. Instead, we conduct one single examination for all grades.**

2. **The exam period is from May 20 to June 10. You may be evaluated at any time during this period.**
   Book your desired date and time in advance.

3. **The exam will be on individual expression of one's ability, in any format.**
   You may present a piece of work, conduct a general presentation on your achievements, or put on a performance. It is up to you.
   Three judges, active at the forefront of the industry, will evaluate you.

* * *

4. You will be graded, but you will not be penalized based on your grades.

5. However, the impression you make on the judges will affect your future, so remain diligent.

"Yikes, this sounds hard-core..."

The examination sounded brutal. Sure, it wasn't like anyone was going to get kicked out of school for a failing score. And depending on how you looked at it, this might have been easier, since there was no need to cram for different subjects. But in a way, this was far worse than any normal exam.

For a typical high school exam, even if you cut corners, it wasn't going to affect your entire future. As long as you put in the effort for qualifications or university entrance exams, then it didn't matter if you'd made some mistakes along the way. You were still able to make up for it.

But performing badly on this midterm might mean sabotaging your own future. It might not be stated outright, but you could end up with your academic status silently tanking.

"Our homeroom teacher is kinda lax but also surprisingly strict about some stuff. It's like they don't even care if some students fail because they didn't bother to check the portal site."

"I see. Now I understand why you're so nervous about this, Akiba."

Akiba was attending Ryouran High so she could secure a comfortable life in the future. To her, anything that could impact that future was a life-and-death matter.

"But you know..."

I tried to cheer her up, as she looked rather panicked.

"This is only the first exam after our admission, right? Even if your work isn't revolutionary, they won't lower their estimations of you by that much, will they?"

"Ah, you just don't get it. You don't understand what it's like for creatives in general, do you, Gakuto?"

"Uh, I guess not."

Do YOU understand it? I wanted to ask, but I didn't.

Akiba wagged her finger pompously in front of my face.

"A project needs to have SOUL. A half-hearted composition won't work in the professional world, you know."

"I don't think anyone's expecting a song of that level from a high school student who's still technically an amateur, though?"

"Maybe for dummies who never think deeply about anything. But this school is different. We're expected to create perfect, complete songs that no one can complain about."

"Well, what if the day when you can compose a song like that never comes, huh?"

"Curse you, Gakuto! You'll jinx me!"

Infuriated, she jabbed my ribs with her phone.

"Ouch. Stop that."

"Hey, Gakuto, your abs are surprisingly toned even though you're a cheeky brat who wants to live a cushy life mooching off rich women. Hya-hya!"

"That looks like fun. Jab, jab!"

"Shiika, you're ganging up on me as well?! Hey... Two against one isn't fair... Stop!"

Still roughhousing, we descended the stairs to the basement.

As soon as I set foot on the basement floor, the sounds and the atmosphere around us changed completely.

Purple neon lights covered the floor and walls, and a rhythmic beat was playing. It had the atmosphere of a DJ playing at a nightclub.

I'd taken this class a few times in April already, but it always struck me as a particularly strange class, even at Ryouran High, which had a lot of unique courses. Still, this place seemed to fit the bill for a hip-hop class venue.

Then...

"That looks like fun! Let me join in! Hya! Hya! Hyaaa!"

"Huh? Hey! Three against one is totally unfair... And by the way, you... Ha-ha-ha-ha!"

My abs were screaming as I was attacked by another jabbing finger that came in from the side. Now I was getting hit in the belly button directly, and I couldn't stop myself from laughing spasmodically.

"Gah! Ha-ha-ha! Who…who's doing that?"

"Who are YOU?"

"You don't even know me, and you're trying to attack and tickle me?!"

"I do know you! Well, that one's Shi, and that one's ManaMana!"

The female intruder pointed to Shiika and Akiba in turn.

They seemed to recognize the girl, too. Well, this was awkward. But it made sense. I hadn't streamed a single thing, so why would anyone know who I was?

"Huh? Wait, I think I've seen you somewhere…"

She had pulled her hands away from my abdomen, and I was able to breathe again. I took another look at the girl.

A baby face, with well-distributed facial features and nice makeup. She had a sex appeal that rested in that dangerous twilight zone between youthfulness and maturity.

Long black hair with red lowlights. A cap that suited her perfectly. Her arms, thighs, and midriff were boldly exposed, and her outfit was that of a dancer, suited for flamboyant movements.

It obviously wasn't the school uniform, but then again, at this school, the dress code was pretty much as free as a bird.

There WAS a uniform, of course, but you could accessorize and style it any way you wanted—or not wear it when the mood struck you. Yep, this was definitely a performing arts school, I thought.

Her presence in this room, at this time, meant that she, too, was one of the students taking the Hip-hop Music class. So it would make sense for me to know her. Though my body was here, my mind was usually elsewhere.

"Ah, ah, ah!"

Akiba was the first to react.

"O-Ootsuka! It's Tatsuki Ootsuka!"

"Yay! Correct!"

"Ootsuka... Oh, the top student of the Dance Department!"

It came to me in a flash.

We'd been in this same class the whole time, but I obviously hadn't been paying attention. Her very existence seemed to have slipped my mind.

Now, you'd expect a girl with a strong personal presence like her to stand out, wouldn't you? Boy, I really must have had my head in the clouds during class.

"Oh, you know little old me? That's so sweet!"

"Well, you're practically famous."

"So then who are you?"

Ootsuka was blunt.

Now, I could have taken that the wrong way and gotten offended, but she said it so thoughtlessly, without any malice, that I simply couldn't hold it against her.

I introduced myself in an openhearted way.

"I'm Gakuto Ikebukuro. I'm the older brother of Shiika Ikebukuro, this one right here."

"Oh, Gakkun! All right, all right, well, nice to meetcha!"

Ootsuka gave a double thumbs-up, chuckling.

"Gakkun..."

I mumbled the nickname, rolling it around on my tongue. She'd given it to me completely out of the blue.

Akiba fixed me with a suspicious stare.

"What are you looking so pleased about?"

"Ah, I mean... This is the first time a classmate's been friendly enough to give me a nickname."

"Oh gosh, what a sad loser..."

"Oh, except for cruel nicknames. I've been given my fair share of those."

"You're making it even worse. Ugh, you're so pathetic..."

Great, I was being pitied.

Listening to our exchange, Ootsuka burst out laughing, clutching her belly and trumpeting: "Pathetic! Pathetic! Ha-ha-ha!"

"You two are so funny! But that's to be expected, after you came out with that totally divine song of yours!"

"Oh, right, I almost forgot. You've been dancing to Shiika's song, haven't you? Thank you. You gave us a massive boost in numbers."

"All right, all right. Listen, I enjoyed myself, too! Candy, party, let's study! ♪"

Ootsuka performed a few dance steps while humming the lyrics. They were casual moves but sharp and sophisticated at the same time.

"*...La-la-la!*"

"Awesome! You're on fire, Shi!"

"*La-la-la!*"

Shiika also swayed her body in rhythm with Ootsuka's.

Shiika's dance was like a sea anemone waving its tendrils in the deep ocean. She lacked even the basics of dancing. But Ootsuka didn't point out her clumsiness or make any wisecracks. Instead, she seemed to be enjoying Shiika's moves.

"What is going on here? This is too much for me to keep up with."

"Don't worry, Akiba. Me too."

"Putting Ootsuka's off-the-wall personality aside, what sparked her interest in Shiika?"

"No idea? Probably only the person herself knows…"

I watched Ootsuka cutting a rug and Shiika trying to imitate her.

This was their first real meeting, but Shiika didn't seem shy around Ootsuka at all. Maybe it was because of Ootsuka's friendliness?

Shiika had a serious expression, humming as she copied the steps. She seemed to really like Ootsuka's rendition of "Study, Party, Candy."

But I had no idea why.

So I just went with the easiest conclusion.

"—Sometimes geniuses are drawn to each other, right?"

"Wow. How philosophical. Still, whatever works for you."

"Aw, shut up."

To be honest, after seeing a nasty display of jealousy from a prodigy (by the name of Erio Shibuya) back in the classroom, I was somewhat relieved to see Shiika interacting so openly with Ootsuka.

Maybe school life wasn't going to be all bad, I thought.

And just like that, we casually became friends with Tatsuki Ootsuka, the top student of the Dance Department.

Erio Shibuya's morning rage was still a shock, but the rest of the day passed without incident.

After second period, we had a few classes with Erio, but she didn't seem to be paying any special attention to Shiika, nor did she approach us.

I thought her minions were radiating a frosty aura, perhaps, but by the time school was over, everything seemed to have already returned to normal.

Matter settled… Was it safe to say that?

Come to think of it, I noticed one thing on the train on the way home after homeroom.

"She's an amateur, a glorified karaoke singer who's not even worthy of licking Erio Shibuya's shoe."

"She actually thinks she's pretty! Gross."

"What'd she do, sleep with the composer in exchange for that song?"

Heartless comments, all over the comment section of Shiika's stream archive that had been viewed one million times.

(Glad I spotted this first. Time to prune.)

To make sure Shiika would never see them, I muted them using my admin privileges.

Why didn't I delete them outright?

Well, that's because there's no way I'll let anyone get away with trying to hurt Shiika.

Just watch, you filthy anon.

I'm going to make you regret this.

◊ ◊ ◊

Squeak, squeak, the sound of metal squeaking. *Hahh, hahh,* the sound of gasps, intermingled together.

It was the last class of the day. The location? The gym, located a short distance from the main school building.

Treadmills, exercise bikes, shoulder-press and lat-pull-down machines... It contained all the standard gym equipment.

While I worked out my lower body on the leg press (building leg muscles by pushing a heavy plate in a seated position), I sneaked glimpses at the other students who were working out in activewear.

The Fundamentals of Muscle Training. Everyone was free to exercise using their own training regimen. The atmosphere seemed much more relaxed than in other classes. In this gym, you could pretty much do what you wanted.

Was this school really okay?

Laziness is the only way! Earning money while indulging in idleness... That was the supreme way of living! At least, that was my philosophy. So an environment like this was perfect for me. It was the others I was concerned about.

In a place like this, only those who took everything seriously could get ahead.

Incidentally, my lazy workout partners, Shiika and Akiba, had quickly gotten tired of running on the treadmill and were now reclining on a bench in the rest area by the vending machines.

Oh well. Shiika's not used to exercise, I thought, extending and retracting my legs with a clunk and a clank.

Then I realized someone was standing over me.

(Hmm? That's unusual.)

The leg press was relatively unpopular, and the machines had remained unoccupied the whole time.

Despite the fully equipped gym, this was a performing arts school. The students wanted to become actors, models, singers, and pop stars, not bodybuilders. Sure, building a nice physique was an important component of looking good, but there weren't many students here fixated on muscles. They tended to focus on the more mainstream, popular exercises like training their abs and backs, running, and the bench press.

…Actually, I only chose the leg press because there were fewer people here. I enjoy being alone. It's my happy place.

"Mind if I use this one beside you?"

"…Huh?"

I didn't expect to be spoken to, and I grunted hoarsely in surprise.

I was even more shocked by the owner of the clear, female voice.

"Um, sure. Go ahead. Wait, what?!"

When I saw the other person's face, I was so surprised that my eyeballs spun 360 degrees in my head.

The girl looked at me curiously, no doubt because of the way I was staring at her with such intensity.

"…Is something wrong?"

"Ah, no. It's just that you're super famous. I was just thinking how lucky I was that you wanted to use the machine next to me."

"Heh. You sure don't mince your words."

She had an air of gravitas in her speech, but she smiled gracefully. Of course I knew her, this girl who exuded an aura of elegance, like she was draped in fine silks and furs. I mean, there wasn't a single student in the school who didn't know her.

Io Kanda.

She was the upperclassman who'd given the congratulatory address during the entrance ceremony. She was the top third-year student and one of the most influential people at Ryouran High. She was a first-rate actress, already getting professional roles.

When I saw her in the auditorium, she'd been wearing the school uniform, but now she was in workout gear. She wore a tube top that covered only her chest, revealing a tight midsection, and leggings that fit her perfectly, hugging the right places. I quickly averted my eyes from her healthy curves.

…Goodness, such a sight could turn me to stone.

"But you're not lucky, you know."

"Huh? What do you…?"

She sat down on the leg press beside me, put her feet against the plate, and adjusted her posture.

Clunk. Clonk. She spoke over the noise.

"It's not a coincidence. I came here because I wanted to talk to you… Gakuto Ikebukuro."

"Right… About my sister, huh?"

With her song surpassing a million views, Shiika's popularity within the school had skyrocketed.

It wouldn't be out of the question for some of the really hard-core students to recognize me as her elder brother.

But I couldn't see anyone wanting to talk to me in particular. What was she after? A collaboration with Shiika, perhaps?

But her response surprised me.

"Nah. I'm not super interested in her. I mean, she's really talented, don't get me wrong. It's you who I'm kinda interested in."

"Me?"

"Don't look so shocked. I'm not trying to hit on you or anything."

"Just so you know, I'll see through any tricks…"

Honestly, my guard was up.

I don't do any of this school's extracurricular activities like streaming. Yet here was a beautiful girl, approaching me and claiming to be interested in me. Was she just teasing me, or was she trying to get close to Shiika with nefarious intentions? Even though I stretched the rubbery mass you might call gray matter in my brain to a snapping point, I couldn't imagine why this beauty would want to talk to ME.

"Ever since I happened to see you on campus, I've hoped we would get a chance to talk. Now seemed like a good time, so I took the plunge."

"Ha-ha. Seriously? I'm a complete nobody. Like, the easiest fish to catch that no one would want to brag about anyway."

"Really? The way you carry yourself, your physique… You seem very sophisticated to me."

"You mean my ex-shut-in, loping gait?"

"You do martial arts, don't you?"

"Yeah, like a total pansy. Chop! Hyaaa! Like imitating something from a comic book. If you call doing kung-fu pantomime like an over-imaginative child martial arts, then…I guess anyone could practice it."

"It looks like you weigh around a hundred and ten pounds."

"Yikes, you can guess just by looking? That's scary… But yeah, about that much."

"At your weight, there aren't a lot of people who could leg press four hundred and forty pounds."

"…Really?"

"Really."

Clunk. Clank. My legs stopped.

No one else was doing the leg press, so I'd had nothing to compare myself to. Was this really that heavy?

"I doubt a shut-in would have that kind of physical strength."

"Well, I AM a shut-in. But I spend most of my time at home doing muscle training in my room. Ha-ha-ha."

"I see, so that's what it is. Interesting… Very interesting."

She sounded convinced, but there was a flirtatiousness to her breathy voice. The sight of her toned abdominal muscles contracting was strangely thrilling.

Don't look. Don't think about it. Be an innocent boy. I tried to lecture myself, focusing instead on moving my legs rhythmically once more.

Seemingly unbothered by a silly matter like whether I was really listening to her, she continued in her singsong voice.

"With my work as an actress, I naturally get into the habit of observing people."

"Huff… Hugh… Hnngh…"

"Basically, people live their lives thinking about what aspects of themselves to display and which to hide."

"Hyuh! Hnung! Huffff!"

"But it's not like we've only got two sides. We're more like dice. We've got at least six sides. Some people are even more complicated than that…"

"Hah! Huff! Hoo!"

"There are some differences, of course, depending on the individual, but most men only show me the same sort of, let's say, 'face.'"

"Huff... Do...hah...they?"

"They want to hide their ulterior motives and showcase their attractiveness. Be it overt or casual, I can clearly see their intentions."

She stopped talking.

I gave in to the temptation to look over and regretted it.

Now I was looking straight into Io Kanda's translucent eyes.

"But you're completely the opposite."

Narrowing her eyes charmingly and giving me a big smile, she removed her legs from the leg press plate, turned in her seat, and wiped the sweat off her neck with her towel.

"You show your ulterior motives and stubbornly try to hide the fact that you work out. Consider my curiosity truly piqued."

"Hah... You're weird, you know that?"

"Well, thanks very much."

"I mean... It wasn't a compliment..."

"I think you're weird, too, so maybe that means we can indulge each other's...curiosity."

"Yikes, what a conclusion to leap to..."

"If I see you around at school, is it okay if I talk to you like this again?"

"Just please don't be obvious about it."

"So you mean you'd be willing to meet in secret? All right, roger that."

She was twisting all my words.

I was slightly annoyed and wondered what the heck was going on.

It almost seemed like she sought me out and was trying to get closer to me, but I considered her as someone I shouldn't let my guard down around.

At the same time, she's probably the single most influential person at Ryouran High. If I got on her good side, it might really work to our advantage, in terms of both Shiika's future and securing collaboration partners to get those sweet, sweet numbers.

In that case, I had only one possible response.

"I'd like it if you'd become friends with my sister, too, er, Ms. Kanda?"

"Please call me Io. And I will call you Gakuto, okay?"

"But you're older than me. I can't just call you by your first name; it seems so impolite."

"There's no need for social niceties. After all, you're the same age as me, aren't you, Gakuto?"

"Wow… You know everything, it seems."

Even most of my classmates, the unobservant ones, weren't aware of that.

To think that she's investigated me this thoroughly… I felt more afraid than flattered.

"I've got this fixation with knowing everything about people. It comes with the career choice."

"Right, but I think you're taking it too far…"

"Well, Gakuto, I hope you and I become good friends. Very good friends."

Interrupting my retort with an innocent sort of smile, Io got to her feet.

I gave up, sighing.

"Yes… Nice to meet you, Io."

"Yeah. Well, I'm off."

Never breaking her smart demeanor, Io turned around, her back facing me, and glided off. *Clunk. Clonk.* As I watched her go, I went back to doing leg presses.

How do I explain this encounter to Shiika and Akiba…? Ah, it was too much trouble to even think about, so I decided not to.

I could just tell them at some point later on.

◊ ◊ ◊

That evening…

It was ten PM. I was in my room.

After chatting with my gaming buddy, Zeke, I switched off the PC.

"Guess I'll head to bed…"

I almost laughed out loud in response to my own muttering. Going to bed before the clock hands pointed straight up… Ah, I'd been influenced by my school life.

When I was a shut-in, ten PM was when the day really kicked off. Shiika, too, was another habitual offender of the same crime of staying up late, but now… There wasn't a peep coming from her room. She was probably in her futon already, tucked in and cozy.

"…Huh?"

My phone, charging by my bedside, had started vibrating.

I checked the screen and saw that I had a notification informing me I had a new DM.

But not to my account.

It was a DM sent to Shiika Ikebukuro's Impachi Live account that I'd linked to my phone.

Shiika had no interest in interacting with other people and had left it up to me to check and reply to DMs. It'd been like this since her Way-Tube days, and since we entered Ryouran High School, it'd been the same way with her Impachi Live account.

"Huh?"

I muttered when I saw the sender's name.

Erio Shibuya.

"What does SHE want with Shiika?"

I opened the message very cautiously. Thinking back to the scene this morning…I had a feeling this couldn't be anything good.

If it's a nasty message, what should I do? I was still thinking things like that as I read it…

"Can we meet? I'd like to discuss something important."

Now, that was unexpected.

"What do you want? It's late. Can't we talk at school?"

Without much information to go on, I responded.

The reply came quickly.

"I don't want to talk in public. I'm at the closest station to where you live, so if you specify a place to meet, I can go there right away."

How did she know where we lived?

"Mana Akihabara told me where you live. She coughed it up in exchange for a collab agreement."

Akiba accepted a bribe?! What a heartless wench, to be swayed by Erio's popularity and sell out Shiika and me!

"She didn't tell me your exact address, just the closest station."

"Well, I guess that's all right..."

Actually, it was up to us to decide that, not Akiba, but never mind the fine details right now.

Come to think of it, Akiba was worried about how to survive the midterms. She might have been planning to set up a collaboration beforehand so she could do a presentation saying, "As a composer, I'm working hard to build a business relationship with a top-notch singer!" and pass the exam.

She was doing her best to survive, as a student, so I decided to forgive her. After all, she hadn't divulged our actual address. And she did clean our apartment that one time.

Still, I thought this was very odd.

Any way you sliced it, it was bad manners to call someone out this late and take up their time in the evening. But if Erio had some sort of business with Shiika, I wanted to know what it was. If I turned a blind eye now, and it led to trouble down the road, well...that would suck.

I wouldn't bring Shiika. I'd meet Erio on my own and see what she had to say. That would probably be the best course of action here.

"All right. Come to the park on this map link."

After responding, I changed out of my lounging-around-the-house sweats into a parka.

After checking Shiika's door and confirming there were no signs she was awake, I whispered, "Be back in a bit," and left the house.

◊ ◊ ◊

The children's park at night had a strange atmosphere.

I hadn't noticed it during the day as I'd thought it was just some kind of surreal playground with only one slide right in the middle. But there were plenty of lights, and even though it was a starless night, the park was illuminated with bright-white light.

The vending machines and the public restrooms, which I'd never noticed during the day, now stood out due to the glowing lights they emitted.

This looked like a prime spot for juvenile delinquents to gather. I wanted to head home as soon as possible before I got involved in a strange incident.

A car stopped in front of the park entrance. It was quite a luxury car. I felt like I'd seen a similar scene when I came to this park once before. I wondered which one was more expensive, this car or Kei Tennouzu's? Not like that mattered.

Erio Shibuya emerged from the passenger seat. She wasn't wearing her school uniform, but her regular clothes. She wore her uniform with pizzazz, but even her street clothes were extremely stylish. I wouldn't even know where to go to buy clothes like that.

As she approached the slide where I stood, Erio snorted.

"Thought it'd play out like this."

"Really. So you never expected Shiika to come?"

"Of course not. You're her self-proclaimed manager, her elder brother who's gotten special permission to shadow her around the school. If you hadn't shown up at a time like this, you would've been just a weirdo with a sister complex."

"So it was really me you wanted to talk business with all along, huh. What's so important you can't discuss it with me at school? Cripes, you're not going to ask me out, are you...?"

"Ugh! No way! Just the thought of that is enough to make me puke!"

"Gah... You didn't have to go that far..."

Her words were cutting. I was shocked to the core. Her cruelty was made all the worse by her delivery, in that crystal clear prodigy-level singer's voice.

"...Wait, you didn't come here alone, did you? Who's that, your boyfriend?"

I looked at the man who had just gotten out of the driver's seat, my question laced with malice.

Erio looked affronted.

"That's MY manager. He was driving me home from a lesson."

"A lesson? This late at night? Don't you get enough of that at school?"

"If you're satisfied with just the classes at school, then you do you. I, however, am different."

She spoke as if there was nothing amiss, but this amount of time spent honing her craft seemed crazy to me.

She had a tenacity to her, as if she'd much rather die than lose out to any other singer.

"You said manager… Oh, right. Your debut with a major label has already been decided."

"Good evening."

In response to my gaze and murmur, the man in the suit behind Erio bowed.

He stepped forward, offering his business card with both hands.

"My name is Shinpei Nakameguro from Queen Smile. I represent Erio Shibuya."

"Oh, nice to meet you…"

I scrutinized his face as I took his business card.

He was tall and wore glasses. Late twenties, maybe early thirties. Soft voice, polite demeanor, gentle aura. He may have been a manager, but he was also obviously someone from the entertainment world. His close shave was clearly done by a stylist, and he didn't just look serious. He also had the charm of a successful businessman.

"And you're Gakuto Ikebukuro, correct? I've heard about you from President Tennouzu."

"Ah, that old man… So you're pals with Kei, are you? Boy, it's a small world!"

"Oh, no, me, friends with such an important person? Not at all. If the president heard such a thing, he would be infuriated by my impudence…"

Nakameguro scratched his cheek, looking embarrassed, then continued.

"It's a big world, but the entertainment industry is surprisingly small. A little networking through drinking parties, and you can expand your reach to the big names with surprising ease. In response to Erio's selfish demands, I was able to create a situation where I could speak with President Tennouzu…"

"Who are you calling selfish? Information gathering is supposed to be a manager's job."

"That's not in my job description, though? Anyway, what does it matter now?"

Nakameguro looked resigned. It seemed Erio's shrewish ways were giving him a lot of headaches.

"Anyway. I did some digging, to find out where you couple of unruly upstarts sprang from. And what I found out was…"

"!"

I straightened up in alarm. My brain was already whirring with ideas on how I could handle the two people standing in front of me.

If Kei Tennouzu leaked Shiika's true identity as the Vsinger Seeker, that would mean I'd need to view Erio Shibuya as a definite enemy. If she was planning to use this information to threaten or bully us, then I would have to deal with her swiftly.

Now, then… What would her next move be?

"…Nothing. I couldn't find anything."

"…Huh?"

"Not a thing! Mr. Tennouzu doesn't seem to know anything about you two or where you came from! My manager kept on asking, but Tennouzu kept saying, "Isn't she a catch? Go on, tell me what a catch she is." And he wouldn't say anything more! Just what gutter did he pluck your sister out of, anyhow?!"

"Ah… Ah-ha-ha. What gutter, indeed?"

It was in this very park, actually, but why would I tell her that? I fended her off with a smug smile instead.

Dodge and parry, dodge and parry.

"Hmph. Well, it's not like it matters. A completely unknown rival... All the better."

Erio suddenly closed the distance between us, grabbed my shirt front, and brought my face close to hers.

"Let's have a battle."

"What for?"

"Because your presence irritates me. If you lose, Shiika will never sing another Nokia Komae song ever again. Got it?"

"Fistfights are against the law."

"I'm not talking about a physical fight! I'm saying we should compete in the midterm exam and see who comes out on top!"

"But I'm exempt from taking the exam."

"I don't want to compete against YOU! Shouldn't that be obvious enough here?!"

"Of course it's obvious. I'm trying to give you the runaround here."

"Are you...are you mocking me?!"

"Do you really think grabbing me by the collar and challenging me to a duel will make me warm up to you?"

"Tch. Listen, stop yanking my chain. You're getting on my nerves."

Of course, I understood 100 percent what Erio wanted to say.

But I wasn't about to accept her challenge here, with the person directly involved not even present.

"It depends on what Shiika thinks. I can't decide everything by myself."

"Huh? You're the manager; you make all the decisions, right? Don't just wash your hands of it now!"

"Hmm, it might look like I'm pulling all the strings, but you know..."

Taking care of her social media accounts. Coming up with a business strategy plan. Keeping up with her personal care.

Shiika leaves all kinds of things to me, and as a rule, she generally doesn't go against any of my decisions as her elder brother.

But the relationship between brother and sister is an egalitarian one. None of this master-servant stuff.

"I never make choices on Shiika's behalf without her consent."

"…!"

Erio looked shocked. She bit her lip, shoulders trembling. I wondered what she was thinking.

Would she scream at me, like she'd screamed at Komae? I got ready to cover my ears and protect my eardrums.

That's when it happened.

"Okay. I accept your challenge."

A voice said unexpectedly.

Erio, Nakameguro, and I—we all turned around, startled by the voice.

Shiika's hair, washed out by the bright lights, sparkled. She was wearing a baggy, ill-fitting shirt and shorts. No shoes. Bare feet. She looked like she'd just been mugged or something.

Shiika Ikebukuro. For some reason, my little sister, who ought to have been sleeping at home, was here.

"Shiika. You…," I mumbled, dumbfounded.

I was so shocked to see her here that I couldn't find the words.

I was probably more surprised than anyone.

More than anyone else.

No one else could have felt the same level of shock that I felt right then.

Shiika left the house of her own accord. I was the only one with any idea of how unlikely an event that was.

Shiika's shoulders were going up and down, her breathing ragged, like she'd run all the way here.

Even so, she managed to catch her breath, then spoke again.

"I wanted to hear you sing again, Eri, so I opened the Impachi Live app. And you'd sent me a message, asking to meet."

"So that's why you came here. But are you serious about accepting the challenge? It's not like we're going to get anything out of it," I said.

"Get something out of it? I don't understand. Even so…"

Shiika's eyes were shining in the moonlight. Erio seemed fascinated by the golden glow of her eyes.

"Eri, I want you to realize…that isn't your real singing voice," Shiika said.

Shiika had formed her own thoughts, using her own voice.

Tortured in a classroom filled with filthy emotions, Shiika had cut off all relationships with others. She had no other way of interacting with society except immersing herself in solitary creative activities and sharing her work online.

But here she was, taking a step forward, trying to communicate with Erio.

Perhaps going to school had been good for her after all?

Or was there some message she was passionate about conveying to Erio Shibuya?

Maybe it was both.

I had no idea what Shiika's true intentions were. What was she thinking? What was she feeling? If, as her brother, I had no way of knowing, then how could a normal person ever understand?

Even if I can't understand my genius sister's thinking, it doesn't really matter.

If this is what Shiika's decided, then I'll do my best to make it so she can do whatever she wants. She doesn't need my understanding or consent. Call me a freak with a sister complex if you like, but this is my stance as her manager.

"What…what the heck? You don't know the first thing about me or my voice!"

Erio started yelling, clearly mad.

She let go of me and darted toward Shiika, about to grab her instead.

"Calm down, Erio!"

Nakameguro stepped in, holding Erio's arms.

"Don't get violent!"

"I know that! But did you hear her? She's making fun of me!

Undermining all my effort, spitting on everything I've built, with that smug face of hers!"

Despite being restrained by a grown man, Erio continued to struggle, her emotions having gone wild.

Her eyes were wet. Perhaps it was the heat of the moment?

"I'm angry! I'm mad! I'm pissed! I will not accept this! She's gonna regret this!"

"I understand your frustration. Yes, I understand."

"Then let me go! You're my manager. You know how determined I am to get ahead in this world! In a competitive society like this, where it's dog-eat-dog, survival of the fittest, do you have any idea how much time and money it took me to get this singing voice?!"

"I understand. I understand."

"My singing voice… She said…she said it gives her the ick! Do you think she should be allowed to get away with that? No, right?!"

"But if you get mad here, you'll lose everything you built. Erio, those who have the eyes to see it will understand your talent."

Nakameguro looked desperate as he tried to restrain Erio.

For a singer just about to debut, an incident of public brawling would ruin her whole career. The manager would get it in the neck, too. He'd be lucky just to have his pay docked. But depending on how much the company was expecting to earn off Erio, he could end up being fired instead. No wonder he looked so frantic.

In the face of Erio's railing, Shiika spoke, her expression calm and still.

"If I win, you'll try singing in the way I suggest. I would like to do a collab with you, Erio, if you can sing like that."

"Huh? Are you insane? You seriously think, after everything you've said to me, that I—"

"It's just because I'd like to hear it. And I think that kind of voice would suit you much better, Erio."

"…!"

Erio suddenly stopped trying to attack Shiika. But she was still

agitated, with her brow furrowed and breathing rough. Shiika's unflinch-
ing calmness in the face of her rage seemed to have had somewhat of a
cooling effect on Erio.

Gritting her teeth remarkably hard, Erio finally took a deep breath
and calmed down.

Her entire body seemed to go limp.

"You're after my view count, aren't you? All right. That makes sense.
I'm fine; you can let go of me now."

"...All right."

Erio was speaking calmly, and Nakameguro hesitantly released her.

Rearranging her disheveled clothes, Erio looked at Shiika.

"Okay. If you win, I'll do anything, even a collaboration. But if I win,
you won't sing a single one of Nokia's songs. And you'll delete your
stream archive."

"Mmn. All right."

Shiika agreed without hesitation.

Her collab with Nokia Komae had really grown her channel, and
most of her ten thousand subscribers had come from her stream with
him. With that stream archive erased, and no more collabs with Komae,
Shiika would lose momentum. There might even be weird rumors
going around about her after that.

But if that happened, we'd deal with it later. If Shiika was determined
to win, then there was nothing I could do to dissuade her.

"You've got some cheek, haven't you? Just watch. I'll mess up that
poker face of yours."

After spitting out those words, Erio turned on her heel.

Nakameguro followed her as she stormed out of the park.

Just before getting into the car that was parked at the entrance, Erio
suddenly looked back, as if she'd forgotten something, and with a defi-
ant look, she said:

"Make sure to bring a handkerchief on that day. You're gonna want
to cry after being humiliated in front of the judges."

Then she disappeared into the car.

Nakameguro gave us a quick bow before getting into the driver's seat and starting up the engine.

I sighed a little as I watched the car vanish into the darkness of the night.

"Shall we go home, too?"

"Yeah. *Achoo.*"

"Going out dressed like that in the middle of the night… Please don't go catching a cold."

"Piggyback. My feet hurt."

"You should have worn shoes."

Rolling my eyes, I willingly let Shiika hop on my back. I could feel her warmth, and she was light as a feather.

Her bare feet poked out in front of my waist. Seeing them, all scratched up from walking on the asphalt, I felt happy.

Those scratches were signs that Shiika had taken action on her own…however clumsily.

Running out on her own volition. Winning her battles on her own.

She was doing things she had never done before.

That fact alone made me so happy that I wanted to cry.

Chapter 5:
Omnidirectional Lost Ones Catalog

"This is big. This is crazy! Something incredible is underway, so I just had to hop urgently on to live stream! At my humble home, where I always stream from, we have avery special guest! The one you all know! The girl you've been begging for collabs with in the comment section. Now she's here! On this channel! Ah, it's much too much! I'm beside myself with excitement!"

Talking excitedly was a familiar dark-haired girl…Mana Akihabara.

A female friend I saw on an almost daily basis seemed different somehow while streaming.

Maybe it was because she was doing a collab with a genuine star?

"And so it gives me great pleasure to announce that Erio Shibuya has come to hang out with me! All right, give her a big hand, everyone! Don't be rude!"

"Hello. I'm Erio Shibuya. Wow, so many viewers. What a big welcome!"

"Oh, no, no, my channel's still tiny! Whoa, wait—those are my Now Watching* numbers?! That's ten times… No, a hundred times more than what I usually get! Oh! Oh my! Hoo! This is the Erio effect in motion! Unreal!"

Akiba was blushing with excitement over the highest number of viewers in her channel's history. If she was in an anime, she'd have the yen currency symbol flashing in the pupils of her eyes.

Keeping one eye on the video, I grinned and addressed the real Mana Akihabara in front of me.

"You look like you were having fun. Huh, Akiba?"

"Ah… Ah-ha-ha…"

It was lunch break on a weekday in the midst of the midterm exam period. We were in the Ryouran High student cafeteria. Shiika, Akiba, and I were seated at a four-person table in the corner.

Akiba had ordered a high-calorie *yakiniku* lunch, but the ribs and loin that were gorgeously decorated on the plate had been generously divided up, with most of the meat now resting on Shiika's plate as well as mine.

Akiba's obvious desire to atone for her sins with food.

Of course, her crime was divulging the nearest station to the Ikebukuro household to Erio Shibuya.

I didn't get angry right away. I wanted to see if she'd come clean on her own. But in the end, Akiba didn't turn herself in until the day of her collaboration with Erio. Thus, today was the day of reckoning for her.

"I'm… I'm sorry. Please forgive me. Okay?"

"Hmm, since nothing terrible happened, I guess I shouldn't get too mad about this. Listen, I won't even ask you to make amends."

"Oh, you're so kind…"

"But I won't forgive you that easily. It's not like I hate you now or anything, but you crossed the line. I just want you to be aware of that."

"I… I think I was manipulated by a dangerous individual…"

"Did you say something? Sorry, I'm not interested in gossip and bad-mouthing."

"Right! It was nothing! Forget what I said!"

"Nice response. A little too nice to be genuine. But whatever. Since you've given us this good food."

"Thanks! Let's dig in!"

Once she had my permission, Akiba began gobbling up her rice drenched in *yakiniku* sauce.

Rolling my eyes at her, I resumed eating. When I tasted the meat that Akiba had given as a form of apology, the rich, salty sweetness melted on my tongue.

"Oh, this is so good."

"Meat… It's been so long… *Nom!*"

Shiika also devoured it with sparkling eyes.

It had been a long time since we had a good meal.

Since the start of May, our streaming numbers had increased. We had good prospects of earning a decent stipend this month, but payday wasn't until the end of the month. I couldn't let my guard down until I knew how much money would be transferred into our account. This was no time to spend extravagantly.

I chewed on the meat, praying this taste would become a regular thing next month.

"…Hmm?"

Watching Akiba and Erio's collab stream as I ate, it suddenly struck me. There was something strange in the comments section.

"ERIO SHIBUYA IS A PIECE OF TRASH WHO SELLS ONLY BECAUSE OF HER YOUTH AND GOOD LOOKS. HER TECHNIQUE IS BELOW AMATEUR. SHE HAS NO TALENT.

"SHE SUCKED SOME INDUSTRY EXECUTIVE'S (REDACTED), AND THAT'S THE ONLY REASON WHY SHE'S DEBUTING WITH A MAJOR ENTERTAINMENT COMPANY.

"IS IT TRUE THAT SHE MAKES SOCK PUPPET ACCOUNTS JUST TO TRASH HER RIVALS?"

The comments were scattered throughout, but they were all from the same user.

"Hey, don't you think this is odd?"

I showed Akiba my phone, slowly scrolling through the comments section.

Akiba scanned the screen, scarfing down her rice.

"Not really? It's just the usual hate comments."

"But here. Look. Erio having a contract to debut with a major label is undisclosed information, isn't it?"

"Yes, but look at Erio Shibuya's trajectory. Anyone could predict that. There were rumors circulating online that her music video was so good that she already had a major management company handling her."

"Right..."

"What's bothering you?"

"Nothing, just... It sounds like the hater behind these comments might be a little too close for comfort."

"There are haters everywhere. I mean, I've written a few hate comments myself in my time."

"Huh?"

She said this so casually that I was stunned.

Akiba spoke with zero guilt.

"Just for a bit, when I was in junior high. There was this bully who published a song written by someone they bullied, claiming it was their own song. I didn't like that, so I kinda became a bit of an online stalker."

Akiba giggled, like she was recounting a tale of her own heroism. Then her face fell.

"But it's hypocrisy to bash someone online when you can't do it in person, in the classroom. It's just self-gratification at that point. That's why I don't do it anymore."

"I see... A bandit who defeats the thieves undercover. Like some sort of antihero."

"I'm not a bandit. I was just exploiting an opportunity. It's not like I did anything wrong. If you're going to lecture me, I'll take that meat back!"

"No way."

I moved the plate away and easily dodged Akiba's outstretched chopsticks.

"Guh... Well anyway. The industry is extremely competitive, and the classroom is like a microcosm of it. I bet you could find a hundred people who'd love to stab Erio Shibuya in the back. Probably someone's posting hate comments based on classroom rumors. Actually, that sounds totally plausible."

"I see, I see."

In that case, did that mean the individuals posting hate comments on Shiika's videos were nearby, too?

It would be pretty easy to sniff out the culprits, then.

Once I do, I'll deliver swift and painful justice. Oh yes, I'd made my mind up about that.

"By the way, is Shiika going to be okay for the midterm exam? She's going to have a showdown with Erio Shibuya, isn't she?"

Akiba suddenly changed the subject.

"Yeah. Showdown is tomorrow," I answered.

"What song are you guys going to use?"

"We're planning to do a cover of an original song by an online singer, who does a lot of I Tried Singing vids."

"Seriously? You're not going to use that new song that Komae wrote just for Shiika?"

"Apparently not."

"Apparently not; what do you mean?"

"It's out of my hands. This is what Shiika wants. Even I can't guess what goes on in Shiika's head."

I glanced over at Shiika, who was beside me as I spoke.

"*Nom.* Yum."

She was happily devouring the meat, acting like her usual self.

But tomorrow's midterm exam would be a big day for Shiika.

After all...the song she was planning to sing...

Was the first original song by the popular virtual singer known as Seeker.

Shiika would sing her own song. It was kind of a statement. A statement saying she no longer cared if her true identity was at risk of being exposed.

I had no idea what prompted Shiika to make this decision, but it was HER decision. I'd already made up my mind to keep my mouth shut and respect her wish.

◊ ◊ ◊

That evening. I logged onto *EPEX* and started playing a game with Zeke while we chatted on Wizcode.

It wasn't the sort of serious mode where ranking was at stake, just a carefree match where all you had to do was fire your guns at random. We were more focused on chatting.

"Ah, by the way, Lord Gaku-Gaku, the matter you entrusted to me… It has been successfully completed."

"Is that so, Zeke? Thank you for taking the trouble to do that."

"No, no, not at all. It was a piece of cake compared to stealing national defense information on hypothetical enemies."

"That's an odd comparison to draw."

"Ha-ha-ha. So I believe I've identified the source of the hate comments on Impachi Live."

"I see, I see."

"I discovered something quite interesting. I've sent the information I've gathered to your phone."

"Thanks."

Playing the game with one hand, I pulled out my phone with the other.

He'd sent me a detailed research report.

Zeke and I were friends only in the game world. I didn't know his real name or what he looked like. All I knew was that he had a sort of old-fashioned way of talking and that he worked with computers.

Yes, computers… By which I mean his main occupation was a hacker. He was a half-cracked hacker who treaded the boundary between right and wrong.

The other day, I asked Zeke to identify the user who'd left malicious comments on Shiika's streams.

"The ISP of the device used to post the comment, and… Yes, it even has the social media accounts linked to that device. Amazing. It's incredible the things you've found out."

"Well, the target was quite careless. It was easy to track them down. It was almost like they wanted me to catch them."

"Ah-ha-ha, no one's safe from you, Zeke… So what's the interesting thing?"

"Oh, right. The same device belongs to an individual who also streams on Impachi Live."

After a long pause, Zeke continued.

"A popular streamer by the name of Erio Shibuya."

"...I see."

I wasn't surprised to hear the name. Judging from Erio's attitude toward Shiika, it wasn't shocking to find that she'd be using sock puppet accounts to post hate comments. Yes, she'd been a very plausible suspect.

"But here's where it gets interesting. Erio Shibuya has apparently been writing hate comments on her OWN streams—and streams of those she has collaborated with."

"Huh?"

I was astounded and got distracted, and just then I took a sniper rifle bullet to the head. Yikes, dead in the early stage.

"Hey, hey, eyes on the screen."

"Sorry..."

Though I apologized, thoughts continued to run through my mind.

Erio Shibuya, writing hate comments on her own streams, from a sock puppet account created by her.

What for? What was the point of that?

I knew she hated Shiika. Her reasoning... Well, pick one. Jealousy, anger, a desire to crush her rival...

But there was no reason for why she'd be posting hate comments about herself. Maybe it was some sort of trick, trying to draw pity by making it look like she had petty haters? An attempt to inspire fans to protect her, to solidify her core fan base?

But Erio Shibuya never responded to hate comments and maintained an aura of detachment. Based on Zeke's intel, it didn't look like she was trying to strike up discord using her sock puppet accounts. I still couldn't figure out Erio's true goals. Things were getting murkier and murkier.

"Zeke, do you have any idea why Erio would be doing this?"

"Not as far as I can see."

"Right..."

"Perhaps it is proof that we cannot understand the darkness that lurks in the hearts of young women."

Zeke spoke earnestly. I could hear loud gunshots in the background. There was something pleasing about it. I almost laughed.

Then Zeke spoke again.

"By the way, Lord Gaku-Gaku. During my investigation, something became clear."

"What might that be?"

"The Impachi Live streamer you asked me to look into, Miss Shiika Ikebukuro, was it? That girl... Her singing voice... Is it not a perfect match with the songstress known as Seeker?"

"You're imagining things."

I answered without hesitation.

Of course, I was aware of the risk of him making that connection. But through our gaming sessions together, I felt I knew him well enough to trust him.

"Hmm. Well, it does not matter. You seem to have your own situation going on. It would be boorish of me to pry."

"...Thank you."

If Zeke looked into it seriously, he would have found out about Shiika in no time flat.

But he wasn't the type of person to destroy a friendship just to satisfy his own interests.

Because he was a just and moral person? No, quite the opposite.

Because he was a villain who could instantly satisfy any curiosity he desired, he was therefore not so hungry as to destroy himself with petty curiosity. A man who's popular with girls, and can get a girlfriend any time, won't get hung up over a certain girl. A guy who can steal information won't get fixated on data that could be easily obtained.

I just had to keep one promise.

Never make an enemy of Zeke. As long as we maintained our friendship, no disaster of his making should ever befall Shiika and me.

◊ ◊ ◊

It was the day of the midterm exam.

The day started with an ironic cloudy sky. Even before it started raining, my uniform felt damp, and my steps naturally became heavier. Maybe it was my imagination, but the other students looked the same way.

It was 9:50 in the morning. Today's examination would be held during second period, which was just about to begin.

Many students had gathered in the large auditorium, the one that had been used for the entrance ceremony.

Only ten people could take the exam at the same time. However, since any student was allowed to observe, many people gathered, from freshmen to seniors.

There were a lot of diligent students who hoped to learn something from watching the other students' performances. Wait, no, that wasn't the reason.

No other exam had garnered so much attention on any other day.

There were two main reasons why today's exam had attracted so many people.

One reason was that Erio Shibuya and Shiika Ikebukuro, the two prodigies of the Music Department, were taking their exam together. Their spat in the Vocal Basics class had become a hot topic of gossip among the students and had now spread throughout the school. No doubt it would attract a lot of attention if the two were to be evaluated at the same time.

The second reason was that the judges themselves were very popular.

Three judges sat in the front row, in front of the auditorium's stage. The lineup varied depending on the day, but it seemed that today's trio was particularly popular among young people.

"Gah-ha-ha! All these eyes watching, wow. I must be too popular for my own good, huh?"

It was a big, bearlike man with a scruffy face, chewing peanuts with the shell on and laughing heartily. His name was Touyo Oomuta.

A legendary artist who made a name for himself as the guitarist and vocalist in a rock band famous for death metal and shouting vocals. Fans had a soft spot for his habit of wearing bathroom slippers out and about, and they called him Old Fart Level 100.

"Wow, you're the optimistic type. Can you share some of that cheerfulness with me, too? Ah, I'm so unlucky. Oh, when will I find happiness?"

Sighing, head propped in one hand, the woman beside him was

beautiful, with a sorrowful air and a sexy, mature aura. She was wearing a dress that exposed her cleavage. Her name was Hamako Ebina.

A world-renowned jazz violinist, she was considered some sort of world-saving Joan of Arc, sent to safeguard the future of Japan's jazz violin world, as the number of violinists declined each year. At the same time, she was known for her low self-esteem, and one day, when she reached her mental limit, she was heard to remark, *"Who are you calling Joan? Please, won't someone save me?!"* Which became a well-known meme.

"Ah yes. But perhaps these kids aren't here to see us. Perhaps they're here to see Kushiro?"

"Hmm! I think you could be right! After all, he's a pop star who can make anyone's heart flutter. Yep, no one can beat Kushiro!"

"Ah-ha-ha… Both of you are exaggerating. I still have a long way to go."

The man who answered smartly, holding a porcelain cup, was a gentle-looking, handsome fellow with semi-long gray hair and a black glove on his left hand. His name was Reiri Kushiro.

He appeared younger than the other two judges, but it was clear from his career history that he deserved to stand alongside them. He began as a child actor at the age of seven, then at the age of thirteen, he became the vocalist of a male idol unit at a superlarge agency. At the age of twenty-three, he announced the dissolution of the group and his own solo project at their tenth-anniversary live performance. He's been active under a private agency since then and was currently twenty-seven. When he was still working as an idol, he attracted many fans with his stunning dance moves and vocals. As an actor, he appeared in many dramas, movies, and commercials. In addition to that, he had ten million subscribers on WayTube. On the international stage, he was a highly active superstar who was gaining fans in Southeast Asia and North America.

On top of all that, he was said to have a great personality, as well. There were a lot of guys out there who were jealous of him and secretly wished horrible ailments on him, like halitosis or incurable athlete's foot. I could kinda understand how they felt.

So this is what he looked like.

No wonder the students flocked to the auditorium to catch a glimpse of this superstar.

The students taking the exam looked nervous, perhaps because there were so many people watching.

Only two of them appeared calm.

One was Erio Shibuya.

She was gazing at her phone, checking the sound level on her headphones, not even looking at the judges at all.

It seemed she was double-checking the lyrics and vocal arrangement before her performance.

Her expression was solemn. It was proof that she was approaching this with the right amount of seriousness.

The other was my little sister, Shiika Ikebukuro.

"Gak. This is bad."

"What's wrong, Shiika? Are you nervous?"

"The slug I just found is exhausted."

"Hand it over here before the performance starts. I'll return it to its original place."

I grabbed a leaf with a slug riding on it from Shiika.

It had emerged after sensing rain. Then it was plucked up by a human and brought to this large auditorium. What a shock to the senses. Poor li'l guy.

Even though Shiika was my sister, it was still a little gross to think that she'd pick up a slug to carry around and care for.

And right before a very important exam. Right before a major battle.

In this kind of situation, where you could hardly blame a person for running to the bathroom with a stress-induced stomachache, being this laid-back… Well, that was just fine.

(Not that Shiika had any reason to be nervous anyway.)

After all, she didn't know a single celebrity, either from TV or WayTube.

No matter how famous a person may be, they were considered normal in the eyes of anyone who didn't know who they were.

The WayTube videos Shiika watched were things like nature documentaries. Mysteries of the natural world. Animals. Or videos that had nothing to do with human beings, like philosophical explanation videos or reproductions of physics calculations in 3D.

A normal singer would have suffered from a lack of immersion, and their musical expressiveness could have been affected as a result.

But for Shiika, who never had a choice but to deal with the onslaught of all kinds of sounds since birth, keeping a measured distance from musical content was actually the right balance.

Just then, a bell rang. The lights in the auditorium grew dim. There was a hush, like before a movie screening, and the audience fell silent, the excited chattering melting away.

"It's time. Can you go by yourself?"

"Yeah. I'm going."

"Right. Good luck."

After that brief exchange, Shiika jumped up from her chair and walked onstage.

The only ones left in the spectator seats were the slug and me. And...

"It's finally time, huh?"

"Are you going to be rooting for Erio? After all, she was the best collaborative partner, wasn't she?"

"Like I keep saying, please forgive me for that... Obviously, I'll be rooting for Shiika."

"Sorry if I'm having trust issues when it comes to you."

"Shiika is my friend! Erio is my business partner! Both are important, but if I was asked to run over one with a trolley, I would choose Erio Shibuya without hesitation!"

"Wow, can we unpack that?"

Next to me was Mana Akihabara, who always reacted in amusing ways when I needled her about her traitorous collaboration.

On her other side, there was someone else. The key person overlooking this entire operation.

"Who will you be rooting for, Komae?"

"Gakuto, has anyone ever told you that you have a terrible personality?"

"Well, that doesn't bother me."

"So people do tell you that. Makes sense."

The red-haired, handsome Nokia Komae gave a wry smile and an eye roll. He was the one who'd sparked this strife between Shiika and Erio.

Having two girls fight over him and his songwriting abilities... The jerk. If this had been a tug-of-love situation with Shiika as the prize, I'd have given him a merciless noogie. As her elder brother, of course. But this was about artistry, creativity. So there was room for a little bit of extenuating circumstances here.

You'll live, but only by a margin, you handsome jerk.

"To be honest, I have mixed feelings. I want Shiika to keep releasing songs, and I want her to win."

"Right?"

"But thinking about the aftermath, if Erio loses... I mean, that gives me pause."

"The aftermath if Erio loses? I mean, you'll just collaborate with Shiika, won't you?"

"It'd be good if that was the end of it, but..."

Komae's words had heavy implications, and his gaze was downcast. After quickly looking around, he made eye contact with me and lowered his voice. "If Erio loses in public, it will damage her brand. Her reputation as the most talented girl in our year—that she painstakingly cultivated—will be dashed."

"Well, yeah."

"How do you think the other students will treat a queen bee who's lost her crown to a usurper?"

"Oh, come on. Are you saying she'll be ostracized from the female student body? Those girls are as thick as thieves. Like a sisterhood, right?"

"I mean, let's hope so... Those girls may be fickle, but they're still Ryouran High students. Girls who follow the queen bee around like little workers... Compared to normal fans, they're a prideful bunch."

"So you're saying they'll freeze out Erio? And Erio will become a social pariah? They'll kick a girl when she's down?"

"It's highly likely."

Komae spoke quite emphatically.

"Of course, they'll maintain a friendly facade. But under the guise of friendship, they'll attack her weaknesses. Little snide remarks that she's not sure are worth taking seriously. And at the same time, the number of hate comments will increase."

"You sound pretty confident; what are you basing this on?"

"Nothing in particular. I just know it. The girls are all like that at this school."

Komae spoke coldly.

A playboy womanizer. That mask had peeled away, and I was able to catch a glimpse of his real personality.

I felt like one of my questions about Komae had been resolved.

He may look like a handsome guy who's experienced with women, but the way he reacted toward Shiika was far too naive. Perhaps Komae actually didn't have all that much practical experience with romance.

So he aimed to become an entertainer, improving himself, competing with others, and attracting the attention of tons of girls. I felt like I'd seen something a little shameful, something I didn't want to see.

He was attracted to Shiika, but not in a romantic way. It was more like he admired her for her transparency, for not being like the other girls.

Komae himself might have been unaware of it, but if he was in love with anyone, it was...

"Erio is such an idiot."

"If she hears you say that, she'll bite your head off again."

"Well, she is. She's stupid enough to think those hangers-on are actual friends. Showing off her skills and achievements without worry. Honestly believing that those savages will be happy for her."

"Oh, come on. You make this place sound like a den of wolves."

"Well, just look. See that girl filming the stage with her phone?"

"Yeah... I've seen that girl in class. She's one of Erio's cronies."

"And that's Erio's phone."

"Huh?"

"She's fine with lending her phone to her friends. To record dance lessons, to take photos at scenic locations, or when they go to nice cafés. She hands her phone over to whoever's available. And now she's asked one of them to film her midterm exam."

"Why hand over her own phone? Why not just have a friend get the footage, then send it later?"

"Erio's phone is a high-end model with a high-performance camera. She earns the most money, so she can afford something like that. And she says it takes the best pictures and footage."

"So that's why she has her friends use it... But these days, a person's phone is as personal as, say, their wallet."

"That's why I'm saying Erio's stupid."

Komae looked at the stage with pity. There were ten chairs lined up onstage. Erio Shibuya was sitting in one, waiting for her turn.

"She's like some dumb, wild boar that just trusts its surroundings and charges forward. That's fine, as long as she's running at the head of the herd. But if she hits a wall and falls down...then she'll become food for the hyenas in no time."

"Hmm, I think I understand."

"Sorry. It's got nothing to do with you, Gakuto. Erio's been really hostile toward you, so I don't expect you to sympathize with her."

"Well, I'm not really interested in Erio as a person, so I guess I don't care."

"Right. Anyway, just forget this whole conversation."

"I truly don't care about her, though. I don't hold any grudges."

"Huh?"

Komae blinked, as if unable to figure out what I meant.

"If someone's an enemy to Shiika, I'll crush them. If they're an ally to Shiika, I'll love them. If they're neither, they don't even exist to me. That's my philosophy," I said clearly.

"Gakuto..."

After finding out that the hate comments on Shiika's streams were posted from Erio's phone, my sympathy for Erio had tanked. But Komae's testimony had just given rise to another possibility.

What if one of Erio's so-called friends was the one posting the hate comments, using Erio's phone?

If that was the case...I figured I could hold off on declaring war on Erio.

At least until I figured out the truth.

Of course, I'd let Shiika win this midterm exam competition first.

"Well, the results will come soon. Whether it'll be tears or jubilation. All we can do is watch."

"Heh-heh. You're right. You're right, Gakuto."

Komae turned to look at the front, his face more relaxed now.

I readjusted my position.

Now, let's see. Let's see how serious these two vocal prodigies really are.

That was when the mood in the room changed.

Beside me, Akiba poked my side and coughed pointedly.

"What are you doing? How rude is this—you're getting all chummy with another guy and ignoring the girl who's sitting right between the two of you?"

"Oh, Akiba. Could you be a dear and go toss this slug outside for me?"

"Hey! You're cruising for a bruising, mister."

I was getting comfortable around Akiba now.

I mean, it was just a sign of the deep trust that we had, right?

◊ ◊ ◊

"I felt you were a little stiff. You're relying too much on your superficial techniques. You should train your core more. I'll give you sixty points this time, but please do your best in the future."

"Th-thank you, Mr. Oomuta!"

After giving her dance and vocal performance, the female student exited the stage, bowed low, and left after receiving her evaluation card from the judges.

It was my first time seeing a midterm exam in progress, and now I knew how it worked.

When their turn was called, a student would go to the center of the stage and show off their ability. Any method was acceptable. Students who needed instruments were allowed to bring them. And by applying in advance to the sound technicians waiting in the auditorium, they could even perform to prerecorded music. The screen could also be lowered to display video clips or other presentation materials.

Once their presentation was over, they would leave the stage and approach the judging panel. Then, after listening to a few of the judges' comments, they would receive a card with a score on it and leave the auditorium.

It seemed one had to achieve three hundred points, a hundred from each judge, in order for it to be considered amazing. But a hundred apparently wasn't even the highest score you could get. The jazz violinist Ebina even gave one student 115 points.

In other words, if two contestants showed a clear difference in ability, it was unlikely for them to tie at three hundred points.

One way or another, either Erio or Shiika would come out on top.

A single girl stepped onstage without letting the slightest bit of stress show on her face.

Erio Shibuya.

Do people with talent attract people just by being there? Her appearance onstage was exceptional compared to any student so far. Just adjusting the height of the mic stand and doing some final warm-ups for her voice, she looked incredibly beautiful.

Was it her clothing style? Her posture? She had that hidden X factor. Just by existing, she attracted attention with a power akin to the force of nature. A natural disaster, like a tornado, perhaps.

With her gray-dyed hair and pink underlay, her earrings, her choker—the adornments that covered her entire body—she seemed to radiate "I am a supernatural being. I am different from you" energy.

No other student was so aware of how they came across.

I appreciated that now.

Since I sent the virtual singer Seeker out into the world, along with Shiika herself, I knew the pressure that came with having many eyes upon you. So I could understand it.

Erio Shibuya believes that looks are all you need.

But she doesn't mean it literally.

She had the "look" of a star named Erio Shibuya.

The Erio Shibuya "look" was the important thing.

Like a walking billboard for her act, perhaps.

She must have been nervous. For her, this was a decisive battle, with something important at stake.

She must have had butterflies. She was performing in front of industry leaders who'd achieved the results she was aiming for.

She must have been anxious. Onstage, anything could happen. One mistake could ruin everything you've built. There's no guarantee it would all go according to plan.

She must have been feeling all these emotions.

But so what if she was?

As long as she had the right look…was wearing the Erio Shibuya persona…then all she had to do next was sing.

It was because of her dedication to that persona, her affinity for it, that she was able to command such an impressive presence.

"Well then, please begin."

"Yes. Music, please."

Music started playing in the auditorium, and Erio nodded to the rhythm. Then…

Sound surged like a rising storm.

Starting with a unique low-pitched intro, her voice quickly transitioned into a high-pitched tone. Her singing voice, which freely changed from high to low to match the intense guitar and drums, overwhelmed the auditorium.

Just listening to it made me shiver from the intensity of the sound, and I broke out in a sweat, like I was doing a mild cardio exercise.

"Whoa! Even my bone marrow is vibrating!"

"Her voice... It's soul-piercing. Oh, it's so impactful! I could get addicted!"

"Ah, this is quite amazing."

The three judges were also overwhelmed by Erio's exceptional singing voice. The students, who had gathered in the auditorium with various thoughts in mind, had their wicked opinions and distractions blown away—and had no choice but to listen with admiration.

Chest voice, falsetto, mix, whistle voice. She used them all freely.

With a vocal range of six octaves as a weapon, singing up-tempo Japanese rock with a high degree of difficulty, Erio resembled Lu Bu, warlord of the Three Kingdoms, charging into battle on his faithful steed, Chi Tu.

This was truly the gem in the crown of Erio Shibuya's singing technique.

She sang flawlessly until the end, and when the music finally faded from the speakers, a kind of anxiety sprang up in my heart. It wasn't just me; I was sure. This was a phenomenon that everyone else was experiencing simultaneously.

The contrast between the roar of the music and the sudden silence was vast, and I mourned the lack of sound.

After a short delay, applause erupted like heavy rain.

In just five minutes or less, Erio Shibuya had the power to get people addicted to her voice.

This was at a professional level. This was top-notch.

Having proved herself, Erio Shibuya smiled, her face sweaty. She turned toward Shiika, who was waiting for her turn, with a triumphant gaze.

How was that? What, no more sassy comments?

That was what her eyes were saying.

"So moving! Absolutely superb! You're number one! Have a hundred and twenty points!"

Touyo Oomuta welcomed Erio as she exited the stage, his jaw working around a mouthful of peanuts with the shells still on.

"Your passionate singing voice is wonderful. If I had a flower like
you in my life, maybe even I could find happiness... One hundred and
thirty points."

Hamako Ebina praised Erio's talent with an enraptured look on
her face.

"Thank you."

Shibuya bowed with a confident expression as she received her evaluation cards from the judges.

Focusing on one of the cards, Erio stiffened.

"Um... Excuse me, Mr. Kushiro."

"Yes, here you are."

Waving a gloved hand, Reiri Kushiro smiled brightly.

Her eyes scrutinizing his face, Erio said:

"You...you meant to give me ninety points?"

"Is there a problem? It's the highest score I gave today, and I think
I'm evaluating your ability properly. The other two can easily give over
a hundred points, but my motto is: If it's not a hundred percent perfect, I won't give a hundred points."

"Could you give me some advice on what I was lacking?"

"No. And I don't think you should ask."

"Huh?"

"I wouldn't want you to take my opinion to heart and change yourself unnecessarily. You've got plenty of talent. You could make it as a
pro. Isn't that enough?"

"Oh... Right. Well. I understand. If you say so."

Shibuya still seemed to want to say something but withdrew instead.

She didn't leave the auditorium, though. Instead, she leaned against
the wall and remained, looking up at the stage. It seemed she intended
to keep an eye on Shiika's exam in order to confirm the results of their
little challenge.

Touyo Oomuta gave her 120 points. Hamako Ebina gave her 130

points. Reiri Kushiro gave her ninety points. Erio Shibuya's total score was 340 points.

Come on, Shiika. Can you surpass that incredible score?

I could hear someone gasp. Fired up by Erio's performance, everyone's hearts were pounding in anticipation for more excellent music. The bar had been raised for Shiika.

Give it to them, Shiika. Melt all their brains. Helplessly addicted to aural pleasure, Shiika was the focus of the audience now.

Yet...

"What is she, some sort of amateur?"

"Sloppy clothes. And her bangs are too long; you can't even see her face. What a pathetic display."

"Right after Erio Shibuya... What a letdown!"

Voices of disappointment begin to rise from the surrounding students, and a smoldering, negative atmosphere began to spread through the auditorium, as if one audience member after another picked up the melody and continued the round.

Of course. Compared to Erio, who exuded a special aura just by standing onstage, Shiika looked like a normal high school girl who just woke up after falling asleep in her uniform.

Her uniform, sloppy and untucked, her hair a bird's nest.

It was Shiika Ikebukuro in her purest form.

She'd been evaluated on the internet many times as a Vsinger, but Shiika had never performed onstage in person. She had no experience to draw from. She had never given any thought as to how to charm the audience as "Shiika Ikebukuro."

There was no way she could reach the level of Erio Shibuya.

The expressions of the judges also seemed somewhat flat. There was not even a shred of anticipation in their eyes, as there had been when they stared at Erio.

"Well then, please begin."

"Hmm... Music, okay."

Shiika waved her hand lightly to cue the music.

A song started playing in the auditorium. Shiika opened her mouth just a little.

Then...

Everyone in the auditorium...

Yes, the judges and Erio Shibuya, too...

They all opened their eyes wide, fixated on Shiika.

◊ ◊ ◊

"H-hey, Gakuto. This song... It's by some online singer, isn't it?"

Akiba, her mouth gaping, turned to me in bewilderment.

"Oh, yes."

"But... This is... Can't put it into words. It's like..."

"Like this song seems made for Shiika herself?"

"That's it! I don't know how to describe it, but it's like you can see a picture in the music. If the song is the background, then Shiika is the girl depicted there. Shiika's vocals... They seem almost...almost as if they're PART of the song itself."

"Wow, you're intuitive."

I said that to try to throw her off the scent, but Akiba's intuition was right.

This song WAS made for Shiika. To be precise, it was made for Seeker, the Vsinger.

And that's not all.

This was an original song, not a song someone else had written for her.

It was Shiika's composition.

One week after the day when a girl named Shiika Ikebukuro decided not to attend school any longer, this song was created in a corner of a dark room that she never once left. The lyrics, the music, the singing, the debut song that Shiika created all by herself.

"Omnidirectional Lost Ones Catalog."

Shiika sees colors in sounds.

And she sees images in songs.

What I mean is that Shiika can paint pictures with songs.

If so, why didn't Shiika do more original songs? Why so many covers? Wouldn't she earn more money through her own songs? You might be asking.

The answer is simple. For Shiika, composing and writing lyrics is like opening a box of memories and emotions that are locked deep in her heart.

Whether beautiful or dirty, good or bad, there is no distinction between them, and she has to look upon them all as a whole...a death by a thousand cuts.

Each note drains her mind, each verse brings pain, and by the time she completes a song, her mind and body are burned out, and she becomes like an empty shell.

Immediately after completing "Omnidirectional Lost Ones Catalog," Shiika was emotionally unstable for about two weeks. She was on the path to self-destruction, with sudden bursts of crying and cravings for unhealthy foods. Somehow, I managed to bring her back from the brink of collapse.

Music is the best form of self-expression possible for Shiika, since she cannot mix well with society. But at the same time, it's a deadly poison that can destroy her. That's why there are only a few original Seeker songs. Basically, the reason Shiika did so many I Tried Singing covers is because it was the best way to maintain a healthy sense of distance.

Of course, there comes a time when Shiika's own feelings of excitement build up, and she wants to compose a song. In such cases, I have no choice but to be on high alert and do everything I can to support her and handle damage control.

But in exchange for all that trouble and strife...

Shiika creates songs by literally shaving off pieces of her life essence. And these songs have a true magic to them.

"..."

"..."

Everyone, from the judges to the students, was fascinated by Shiika's world playing out before them.

Shiika, initially despised, was now being viewed as one of the elements that make up a piece of art.

Because this song expressed who she was. It was distilled from the life force of Shiika Ikebukuro herself.

The way Shiika appeared... It was appropriate. It was the persona that matched this song exactly.

Shiika's song didn't have the kind of stunning power that Erio Shibuya displayed.

But her song had the power to build landscapes inside the minds of all who listened to it.

People are most moved by stories they identify with personally in some way.

It's the same for any beautiful piece of music, any splendid painting. If a piece of work doesn't contain even a thin thread of connection to the heart of the appraiser, then its value will be overlooked. Even classical art, which is highly regarded for its historical value, draws only an "oh, isn't it beautiful?" from ordinary people who don't know the history and context of the field. And a second later, they've already moved on to a different conversation. "So what shall we have for lunch?" and so on.

That's why art that's in tune with the times is always most appreciated by the people of that era.

Like Shiika's song.

Evoking deep emotion.

When I suddenly came to my senses, I found myself clapping, just like the audience around me.

The sound of thunderous applause. I wondered what colors Shiika could see in this auditorium.

Shiika stepped away from the microphone, staring blankly at the audience for a moment.

Her golden eyes were large and puffy, and her white cheeks were tinged a faint red.

It was her first time onstage since she started making music. A live performance in front of a live audience.

It wasn't in front of a real audience of paying guests, perhaps, but it was a private stage with students, teachers, and guest judges of Ryouran High watching. The intensity of the students' gazes and the voracious nature of their applause... It was comparable to that of a full-fledged live performance.

Even Shiika, who lived her life with blinkers on as much as possible, must have felt it, in her heart, somehow.

After standing stunned for a while, Shiika let out an "ah..." as if the realization had just hit her, and she bowed quickly.

Almost stumbling, she made it off the stage and headed to the judges. Then she received her evaluation cards.

"That was amazing...! This is a song you wrote yourself, isn't it? It must be, to be so expressive! You know, I've always felt that life is harsh, but with music like that, it might be worth it after all. Huh... I think this may be the first time I've ever felt that way... A hundred and fifty points. The maximum score possible... You deserve it."

"Gah-ha-ha! So naive, Hamako! I could have done with just a little teensy bit more, so I docked some points. I'm giving the girl a ninety-five!"

Are you serious? I almost had an aneurysm.

Ninety-five from Touyo Oomuta, one hundred and fifty from Hamako Ebina. Two hundred forty-five points so far. Their scores combined were higher than the total amount Erio had received from the same judges.

I was surprised with how low Oomuta's score was. He seemed to appreciate Shiika's ability and talent, but maybe he lacked empathy compared to normal people. Actually, this was a weakness he and Shiika both shared. There's a limit to how much you can move someone with an immovable heart. We couldn't expect a high score from someone with an iron mind like his.

But someone like Ebina, a true empath, was always more likely to give Shiika a high score. So it was a trade-off.

Kushiro was the only judge left.

How would he evaluate Shiika, with that cool smile of his?

I held my breath and watched.

After bringing the white porcelain teacup to his throat and wetting his whistle, Kushiro prepared to speak.

"I won't say too much. The song was a perfect fit for you. A hundred points."

"Oooooooh," the crowd roared.

Touyo Oomuta, ninety-five points. Hamako Ebina, 150 points. Reiri Kushiro, one hundred points. Total score, 345 points.

And Erio Shibuya scored 340.

"She did it, Gakuto! Shiika won!"

"Yeeeahhh!!!"

Akiba and I gave each other high fives.

Even the slug, which I'd forgotten all about, waved its eye stalks jubilantly. Er, maybe.

"I've gotta report this on my stream! Gakuto, can you arrange an interview with Shiika for me?"

"It's a million yen per appearance."

"That's expensive! You think I'm some kinda big-time new network?!"

"Ah-ha-ha. But Shiika's number one in our year now, after all! Witness the crowning of Queen Shiika! Kneel down, fools! Wah-ha-ha!"

"Wh-why are you getting all arrogant? Weren't you the one who said people should be humble if they're at the top?"

"Shiika won't get a big head, so I'm not worried. And I can take a little hate. Bring on the haters! Bring on the malicious comments! If I can earn money without working, then what do I care?! Ha-ha-ha!"

"Geez, you really are trash…"

Akiba's scowl and curses didn't faze me. I was on top of the world!

Then…on Akiba's other side, I spotted Komae's side profile.

"Erio…"

Komae looked worried. He was gazing at Erio, who was kneeling on the floor, hanging her head.

I'd half expected Erio to blow up and go scream at the judges, but that didn't happen. She seemed overwhelmed by despair and was muttering to herself in a stupor like a machine.

"Why…why is this happening…? How could I lose…?"

"Eri."

Shiika had walked over to Erio.

She bent down, looking at Erio at eye level.

"Keep your promise."

"You want me to sing like you tell me to? And for us to do a collab?"

"Yeah."

"Whatever you want… I don't care anymore. And you can do whatever you want with Nokia, too."

"Okay. Now, as for what I want you to do…"

Shiika spoke in a loud, strong-willed tone, so unlike her.

"Don't ever sing in your whistle voice again."

"Huh…?"

"Eri, your natural chest voice is the most beautiful. I see this horrible, horrible color when you use your whistle voice."

"Uh… Ha-ha. So you hate me, huh? Well, I guess I deserve it."

"No."

"But it's true, isn't it? Telling me not to use my whistle voice… That's like telling me to die!"

Erio snarled.

But her expression didn't have the mad-dog intimidation like before. Shiika looked troubled.

"I'm sorry. I just don't think you should sing like that, Eri. I guess I can't explain why properly. I'm sorry…"

"Um, excuse me, mind if I interject?"

Someone had come to intervene between Erio and Shiika.

It was one of the judges, Reiri Kushiro. He lightly raised his gloved left hand, exuding an awkward smile.

"Mr. Kushiro…"

"I wasn't planning to tell you why I gave you ninety points. But it seems that Miss Shiika Ikebukuro noticed it, too."

"Huh?"

"You have acquired a six-octave voice through quite absurd training. Your original singing voice is in a slightly lower range, isn't it? A whistle already puts a strain on your throat. You have no talent for high notes. If you keep using it, you won't be able to sing in the near future. You'll probably have to retire while you're still in your twenties."

"What…?"

Erio seemed at a loss for words.

Kushiro looked surprised by her reaction.

"Oh, you didn't realize."

"I was prepared for a certain amount of risk. But my midtwenties… That's so short…"

"I see, then I should have told you. Thank you, Miss Ikebukuro. I almost made a mistake that could have crushed a genius's career."

"You're…welcome?"

"It's forbidden to discuss the evaluation criteria in front of students, but your health is at stake, so I'll explain and risk my own neck. In this exam, we also evaluate your future potential and the projected longevity of your hypothetical career. The other judges include someone from a style of music where the sound that you produce regularly puts the vocal cords at risk and someone who's lived in the world of musical instruments. So they were able to discount this possible issue. I, however, cannot."

"So you think my career will be done by thirty? And that's why you lowered my score…?"

"Yes. But there was the risk you would disagree and plunge even further down that path. I didn't want to give you advice that wouldn't be helpful to you."

"Right, I see… So, Shiika… You've been worried on my behalf this whole time…"

Erio's voice trailed off, losing strength.

Shiika shook her head.

"No, I didn't know all that. But the color of your voice… It was too forced."

"Color...?"

"Yeah. All the sounds in nature have beautiful colors. Whether they occur naturally or are constructed. But the color of your singing voice was distorted."

"So why didn't you just dismiss me as no good? Why did you try to save me?"

"Because it seemed like a waste."

"Like a waste?"

"Your original voice is a gorgeous color. It just has that bad, distorted color painted on top. I wanted to see the true color underneath."

"Right... I see... It makes sense now..."

Shiika seemed to have expressed her thoughts, however clumsily. As Erio listened to her stumbling explanation, her expression gradually grew more and more morose.

As a third-party observer, I thought it seemed like they were both as clumsy as the other.

Shiika was a poor communicator who stayed locked up inside of herself and kept her words in her own heart.

While Erio was weak at communication and violently expressed her emotions with a barrage of words.

Both of them were clumsy and inept—and only able to convey messages to others through their music. They probably needed this grand battle as an excuse to finally have this conversation.

Erio bowed low before Shiika, still looking morose, seeming like she was struggling to hold back her emotions.

Then, in a trembling voice, she said:

"...Sorry."

"Huh?"

"I'm sorry. I didn't know... I said such terrible things."

Moving forward and burying her face in Shiika's chest, Erio's entire body shook.

Shiika looked up at me with a worried expression, as if she didn't know what to do.

I nodded, and then fearfully, slowly, timidly…

Shiika put her arms around Erio.

Like a mother. Like a sister. Like…a friend.

She hugged Erio and gently patted her back as she sobbed.

"I'm sorry, too. I couldn't express what I meant properly."

"No. It's me. I was the worst. Sorry… Sorry! I'm so sorry…"

Embracing Shiika's small body, Erio sobbed.

The thread that had been pulled tight snapped. The brakes were no longer working. And the tears continued to flow without stopping.

Looking at these two young geniuses, Kushiro smiled and spoke to the other judges behind him.

"Seems like Ryouran High has a good crop of freshmen this year. I'm looking forward to seeing what these kids do in the future."

"Yeah!"

"Yes, indeed."

Oomuta and Ebina nodded, looking satisfied.

Then, hearing the bell ring for lunch break, the three judges got up from their seats and made to leave the auditorium.

"Mr. Kushiro, may I ask one last question?" Erio inquired from behind them.

Kushiro turned and nodded.

"Go on."

"If I hadn't used my whistle voice…would you have given me a hundred points on today's exam?"

There was no point splitting hairs now. Surely she knew that.

But this wasn't a question born from the desire to cling to the past and complain.

But one for the future. It was an inquiry that would help her reconsider the path she should take.

Kushiro answered the young genius's sincere question with a smile.

"I can't say how much the power of your singing voice will drop until I actually hear it… However, from my point of view, even without the whistle voice, I think the expressiveness of your voice is outstanding. Certainly worthy of a hundred points."

"Thank you, sir!"

Erio bowed low. With a flutter of waving hands, the three judges exited the auditorium.

Seeing Shiika and Erio both praising each other for a good match, I sighed in relief.

Maybe Erio would be all right now. She wouldn't do anything to negatively affect Shiika.

I also understood why Shiika had doubts about Erio's voice and therefore tried to tangle with her using Seeker's song.

Erio's real voice had a wonderful color to it, and Shiika wanted to add that color to her box of pigments.

I was glad to see two musical prodigies finding common ground with each other.

Only one issue remained, a trivial one.

"Komae. Can you tell me one thing?"

"Huh? Ah, right, sure. But why do you look so serious?"

"Hearing what Erio said earlier, there's something bothering me..."

I asked Komae a few questions to confirm the suspicions and hypotheses I had.

After listening to his answers, my suspicions became convictions.

The silhouette of the dark shadow that had been lurking around Shiika and Erio had become clear.

After hearing my thoughts, Komae turned pale.

"Seriously? In that case, Erio is..."

"Yeah. She wants to stick with you. That's why Erio is in this position. You should talk with her. Discuss what comes next."

"Un...understood."

"Please do. Now, excuse me."

Saying that, I left my seat with the slug in my hand.

"Where are you going, Gakuto?"

Akiba, who'd been listening to me converse with Komae, piped up then, also looking solemn.

"I'm going out for a bit. I have a troublesome slug that needs discarding," I responded, smiling.

◊ ◊ ◊

The rain was pouring down that afternoon.

Within the vast grounds of Ryouran High School, the outdoor garden, which would have been a place for students and teachers to relax on a sunny day, was now empty except for the blooming hydrangeas. It was far from the school building and other facilities and surrounded by hedges, so no one was even looking in its direction.

I placed the leaf with the slug on it down at the base of a hydrangea bush. *Take care of yourself,* I said.

I wasn't carrying an umbrella. My whole body was already soaking wet, but it didn't bother me.

After all, I'd no doubt get dirty soon enough anyway. Using an umbrella seemed pointless.

I heard footsteps behind me.

"Huh, so you came. You're a coward, but you do have some courage, I guess."

"You summoned me here. Why wouldn't I come? Especially after the threat you made."

"Spoken by someone who's done far worse things than blackmail."

"…Well, I didn't give you my business card with that in mind."

I turned around.

A tall man in a suit and glasses stood there. I could see his face clearly underneath his umbrella. Shinpei Nakameguro from Queen Smile. Erio Shibuya's manager.

I had called the mobile number written on the business card he'd given me and asked the man to meet me here.

What I wanted to discuss was, of course, the small matter involving the constant hate comments on Shiika's streams.

"So you won't mind if I go to the gossip magazines with what you've done? Or pass the information to an influential streamer? Of course, I could just report you to the police. Which would you prefer?"

"Hmm. Before that, could you tell me what you're basing that on?"

"Ah, playing dumb, I see. It's such a hassle to explain. Where do I even start?"

I tapped my finger on my temple three times in rhythm, organizing the information in my head before speaking.

"First of all, as I told you over the phone, I have identified the device used to write those hate comments. It was Erio Shibuya's cell phone."

"Well, now, that would indicate Erio was the culprit. As her manager, that troubles me."

"But in that case, there's something's funny about it."

"What do you mean?"

"The same account also wrote hate comments on Erio Shibuya's streams. Why would Erio write things like that about herself? It doesn't make any sense."

"Perhaps she's been the victim of a duplicitous pal? She often entrusts her friends with her phone to take photos and so on. No doubt it would be easy for them to find a window of opportunity."

"I thought about that possibility as well. But it still doesn't fit."

"Doesn't fit?"

"If someone wanted to frame Erio, they'd stay logged in to her account. If all they wanted to do was write mean comments, they could make their own sock puppet account from their own phone."

"…"

"So I think there was a different motive. Why perform such malicious acts on Erio's device in particular? Perhaps someone wanted to force Erio's hand one day by serving her with a disclosure request."

"What…? Heh-heh. That reasoning's crazy. Even without knowing how the people the comments are about will react?"

"They carpet-bombed people who were likely to grow in numbers, right? There's always someone willing to do something like that. Recently, people are always trying to cancel celebrities for perceived slights. So the chances of getting caught up in something like that are high."

"You're saying it was me, then?"

"Yeah. If Erio hands over her phone to her friends, you can bet she hands it over to her manager when needed. I bet she entrusts you with reviewing her lesson footage and her social media accounts. She's devoted to singing. No doubt she thinks there's nothing on her phone that would embarrass her if anyone else saw it. It's honorable, really, isn't it?"

"But it doesn't make sense. What's the point of me, her manager, doing something that's disadvantageous to her?"

"You wanted to hurt Erio. In a way that wouldn't impact your own career."

"...!"

Nakameguro's expression suddenly changed. I must have hit the nail on the head.

I continued.

"That's why you left hate comments on Erio's channel. Anyway, you kept trying to hurt Erio...to isolate her and make her dependent on the agency."

"Ridiculous. You've got no basis for any of this. What do YOU know about our agency?"

"You're the one who set up the production policy of the Six-Octave Diva and showed Erio how to do it, right? I don't know if it's an organization-wide way of doing things or if it's your personal methodology. It's too demonic to impose a vocal method on someone that could end up wrecking them by age thirty."

Just remembering what Komae had told me earlier made me feel uncharacteristically angry.

"Since when did Erio start having you write such difficult songs, Komae?"

"Huh? Um, I think it started around last year. After she started using Six-Octave Diva as her personal slogan."

"Yeah, but isn't that the agency's production policy?"

"Ah yeah. Since her debut's been settled with that direction in mind."

"Can I ask one more thing? So you're interchangeable, and Erio is planning to pursue an exclusive arrangement with a top-class composer going forward, right? Did you hear that from Erio herself?"

"No, I didn't discuss it with her. I got the feeling it would be awkward to bring that up…"

"Then who did you hear it from?"

"From her manager, Nakameguro…"

Right. Komae was about to be stripped away from Erio at the discretion of Nakameguro.

Regarding the exclusive arrangement… It was doubtful he'd even bothered to get Erio's consent for that.

"Erio, who succeeded in taking on the challenge of six octaves, became an indispensable product for you. But she wanted to hit the big time together with Komae. That was a point of contention. Erio's got a feisty personality, so when she wouldn't listen to reason, you figured you needed to intervene. After all, you spent time and money raising her to be a true diva, so when she wouldn't listen, you were forced to bring her into line."

That's what gave him the idea.

A way to isolate Erio Shibuya, to make her more dependent on the agency, to make her their puppet.

Spread information that would cause a rift between Erio and Nokia Komae. Force them apart. Then gradually drive Erio into a corner. And finally…

"The disclosure requests and lawsuits. She could deny it all she liked, but data would prove it was sent from her phone. She'd have no excuses. A drastic thing to do, perhaps, at a very vital stage, but the agency wanted Erio cornered, as well."

"Enough to damage her value as a talent? That's idiotic. That's too high-risk, low-return."

"That's why you kept it small-scale, didn't you?"

"…"

"A student at Ryouran High School. A streamer without an agent, whose influence has just begun to grow. That way, you wouldn't infringe on the interests of other companies. Yes… With that kind of target, even if it leads to a lawsuit, you could easily get rid of them with settlement money and some mild persuasion. If it's a major law firm, on the other hand, they'll understand the litigation process. It'll be risky. I... Gack! ...Yikes, I think I've been talking too long."

I wasn't used to long speeches. My decrepit vocal cords from being a shut-in were being stretched like old rubber bands.

I'm an ordinary person who doesn't have pipes like Erio or Shiika, and just speaking my mind was taking its toll on me. Guess I shouldn't go pushing myself to do things I'm not used to.

"Anyway, I've figured out everything you're up to. So why don't you just admit it?"

"Hah... To be caught by a meddlesome kid."

Nakameguro rested his umbrella along his nape and shoulders. Then he pulled a cigarette from his chest pocket and lit the tip.

He inhaled, then exhaled a plume of white smoke.

"Don't go bullying a harmless businessman, now. We have to get ahead, or we'll be stuck on a low salary forever. Now, don't you think that's a travesty?"

"What do I care about that, you dumbass? You have a low salary because all you can produce are acts that'll flame out in a decade or so."

"For amateurs, maybe. Real pros keep their star shining bright for at least a decade. All you have to do is ensure they make a fortune during that time frame. Who cares if they flame out after that, as long as a fat pile of money had been made?"

"......What did you say?"

"Take Vsingers, for example. A singer who performs in the guise of a character. These days, even if a flesh-and-blood singer burns out, they can transmigrate into one of those. The Six-Octave Diva persona could continue, even if they're not Erio Shibuya. Smart customers might get fussy over them being the same person, but most people don't care about irrelevant truths like that. I can keep them performing, like nothing's even changed."

"Geez. You're so rotten you're stinking up the joint."

"Hmph. Can't believe I'm talking business with a kid. All right. How much?"

"What?"

"You're blackmailing me for money, right? How much do you want?"

"I don't want money, you piece of trash."

I didn't even hesitate. It's true, my driving intent is to live a life on easy street without having to work.

But more than that, my goal was to eliminate all of Shiika's enemies. This man wouldn't get away with this for the price of a settlement.

"I'll let the police handle you. Anyway, I know you're abusing and manipulating the other acts you're in charge of as well. I'm sure I can dig up as much evidence as I need. You're guilty as sin."

"You don't want a peaceful resolution? Is that all right with you?"

"Yeah. Even without your money, a collaboration with Erio Shibuya could have me rolling in dough."

"That's not what I meant."

Nakameguro dropped his damp cigarette on the ground and threw down his umbrella.

He cracked his neck and knuckles and started taking steps toward me. His light footwork told me that he had some experience in martial arts.

"I'll break two, maybe three bones and pass it off saying you were punched by a passing drunk. An unlucky accident that led to your death. Is that all right with you? That's what I'm asking."

Ah right. So he was choosing violence.

I thought things might go down like this. That's why I didn't bother with an umbrella.

Still, I had zero interest in fighting.

I just want to watch over the life and career of my super-talented sister, Shiika. I don't want her peaceful daily life being threatened. Once I've identified the disturbing shadows lurking around Shiika and I'm on track to eliminate the threat…then I don't need to quibble over the small stuff.

So for now…

And I think we call "cut" right here.

Epilogue

"Shinpei Nakameguro (thirty-four), an employee of the major entertainment agency Queen Smile, was arrested on suspicion of violating the Unauthorized Computer Access Prevention Act. At around five PM yesterday evening, the police received an anonymous call. When they rushed to the scene, a public restroom in Tokyo, Nakameguro was found naked and detained, along with numerous pieces of evidence. It seems Nakameguro has been arrested at this time after the receipt of multiple reports of violations from talents belonging to his agency. The Metropolitan Police Department is proceeding with the investigation and are adding additional charges of intimidation, coercion, and assault. In addition, Nakameguro had bruises all over his body and three broken bones at the time of his discovery and was believed to have been involved in some kind of altercation. This is being investigated as a separate case."

A voice reporting from a WayTube news clip was being streamed in our living room.

Shiika, staring at the phone propped horizontally on the low table, turned her gaze toward me, muttering:

"Did you do this, Gak?"

"I have no idea what you mean."

"Systema, wasn't it? Some sort of martial arts–combat technique?

Gak, whenever you're not online gaming, that's what you're practicing in your room, isn't it?"

"Hey, Akiba! Where's that tuna?! Shiika wants *maguro*! Hurry it up!" I yelled over to Akiba in the kitchen, ignoring Shiika's accusations. Please don't poke any further, Shiika. If this gets exposed, I'll be put in jail for sure.

"You just need to take the lid off the tuna, so do it yourself! I'm making sea bream soup just because you two said you wanted some! Do I have to do everything around here?!"

"You don't want an exclusive interview with the new top singer in her year or what?"

"I'll boycott."

"Darn it! Thank you both! For the collab!!!"

Akiba screamed and went back to making miso soup with sea bream.

"Don't put tears in it—you'll spoil the taste."

"Demon!"

We were just bantering back and forth like that.

Then the doorbell rang.

"Akiba, get the door."

"Move your lazy butt! Ah, whatever. It's open! Just come in," Akiba yelled.

Our house was a run-down apartment with zero soundproofing except for inside Shiika's closet, so we were able to communicate with people outside just by shouting. There was a clatter from the door opening, and I heard footsteps.

"Excuse the intrusion. Wow, it smells good. Soup?"

"Hello… So this is where Shiika lives? It's a bit small. But it looks very clean. About what I expected."

Erio Shibuya and Nokia Komae appeared in the dining room.

We were all here for a reconciliation party, and it also served as a strategy meeting for future collaborations.

"You're lucky the smell of the soup is strong. And if it looks clean, that's because of my efforts. Ah, it's so hard being the unsung hero every time…"

But never mind Akiba's complaints.

Erio and Komae each took one side of the low table. Our place was small, but four could still sit comfortably. Ah, how convenient it is to have a low table. I got the impression there was nowhere for Akiba to sit, but that didn't matter, since she'd be busy cooking. If she got mad, I'd deal with it then.

"Shiika, Gakuto. I'm really, really sorry for everything up until now!"

"I told you; you don't have to do that. You apologized to Shiika yesterday, didn't you?"

"She did. She said sorry A LOT."

"I mean, I don't know what I was thinking. I didn't know myself… I didn't know what was really important," Erio said self-deprecatingly while staring at the surface of the barley tea that Akiba had swiftly served.

"Last year, my manager told me that I wouldn't be accepted in the professional world as I was, so I worked hard to acquire a special singing voice. Once I began, I started to get instant results, so after that, I felt I couldn't back down."

"Honestly, six octaves is a lot. Even Shiika can't do that."

"I could. If I tried really hard."

"No, no, don't try it. I mean it."

"When Shiika criticized my singing voice…I felt like I'd been heading in the wrong direction. Like I'd been manipulated. I'd sensed it all along, but that just blew it wide open. And my relationship with Komae had grown awkward, which made everything worse."

"That was my fault, too… I should have made time to talk with you more seriously."

"No, it was all my fault. I was immature and just wanted to show off the power I'd obtained. So I rejected your song meant to have mass appeal to the crowd. Gosh, I was awful."

"No, I was the one in the wrong. I knew you'd be hurt if I gave that song to Shiika. Because of my own petty jealousy, I…"

"No, I'm at fault!"

"No, it's me!"

"No, I insist! Nokia, you did nothing wrong!"

"Can you stop yelling? You're going to blow my eardrums out with that voice of yours."

"Huh? You're one to talk! You're the one whose voice sounds like Gian from the Doraemon cartoon!"

"You didn't have to go that far!"

"All right, all right, that's enough! The walls are thin here! You'll disturb the neighbors! Okay?!"

I felt compelled to step in and put an end to their argument.

Erio and Komae seemed to shrink before the master of the house.

"Sorry…"

"My bad…"

Good, just as long as we were all on the same page.

"But you two… Even after making up, you act like…like a quarrelsome couple."

"Couple! Cuppy-cuppy-couple!"

Shiika joined in, harmonizing with me. Erio and Komae went bright red.

"No! We're business partners!"

"We're business partners only!"

It was funny, the way they both denied it at the same time, in almost exactly the same fashion. I had to laugh.

Shiika also chuckled. Whoa, that's unusual.

Ahem. Erio cleared her throat.

"Uh, anyway… So I've been doing a lot of thinking. And I've decided to end my contract with Queen Smile."

"Because of Nakameguro?"

"That's part of it. To be honest, I got goose bumps when I heard from Nokia about what he did. I don't think I can get past it. But… But that's not all." Erio laughed. "I have a new dream now."

"A dream?"

"Yeah. To be honest, I'm not sure if this incident was an arbitrary decision by Mr. Nakameguro or if the company was involved."

"Hmm, yes. In truth, there were many talents who were successful with that kind of production policy. In the adult world, it might just be a practice that's tacitly accepted."

"Right. So I was thinking of giving back."

"Giving…back?"

"That's right! With my own individual strength, I'll produce results that are comparable to those of the big agencies that exist today! Just by doing what I want to do, I'll gain the kind of influence that'll make adults bow their heads! I'll show everyone the right way to do things isn't just limited to the methods they espouse! We can succeed, even when we do it our own way. I'm going to prove it!"

Erio clenched her fists with excitement. A flame was burning in her eyes.

Even with a change of direction, her aggressive stubbornness was still intact.

"Wow, that sounds great. Good on you."

"Go for it, Eri."

Clap, clap, clap. The Ikebukuro siblings applauded her.

"Why are you talking like it doesn't involve you?"

"Well, how does it involve us?"

"I need to grow to the point where I've got a first-rate agency trembling in its boots. I need a strategy, right? Neither Nokia nor I have the brains. We can't come up with strategies on top of everything else. And you're fellow Music Department students, aren't you? Not to mention Shiika's got crazy talent. There's no way we won't team up, right?"

"Wait, wait, Erio. You mean… Team up with Shiika and me?"

"Right! And PR expert and strategist Mana!"

"You seem to be discussing some really crazy stuff while I'm in here cooking, but… Eh, sounds good. Count me in!"

"Awesome, Mana. You know just what I'm getting at. And once we succeed, we'll form our own agency. We'll create the best musical units in town! What do you say? Wanna set the music world on fire?!"

"Oh yeah. Um… Well…"

She pushed her face right up to mine, and I found myself looking down. It wasn't just her singing that was breathtaking. She was like a tornado.

It certainly was an interesting prospect. Our position at Ryouran High would be solidified, and we wouldn't need to worry about living expenses for the next three years. No need for me to work, either.

All that sounded great.

It just depended on what Shiika wanted to do.

The more people involved, the greater the danger that Shiika would come into contact with unpleasant sounds. If Shiika didn't seem into it, then sorry, Erio, but I was going to have to decline with a will of steel.

"Gak."

"Yeah? What do you wanna do, Shiika?"

"I want to do it."

She answered with no hesitation.

Then I didn't need to hesitate, either.

"Okay, let's do it. Both Shiika and I are on board!"

"On board!"

"Y-yes!!! Thank you, Shiika! All right…let's do this thing!"

Embracing Shiika and squeezing her like a stuffed animal, Erio was in high spirits.

Crushed by her embrace, Shiika looked annoyed, but only for a moment. Then she looked calm and relaxed, as if she were being rocked in a cradle.

I felt relieved to see the look of happiness on my sister's face.

"All right, everyone, here's the soup you've all been waiting for! Hey, why has no one opened the tuna?! Get out plates! I'll open it, then!"

"It's the expensive kind from the basement floor of the department store, right? Looks delicious… Wait, aren't there only three pieces of fatty tuna?"

"Thank you! Here, Shiika, I saved a piece for you."

"Thanks. Good work, Gak."

"Then I'll take the remaining one."

"Hey! Nokia! That one's mine!"

"You're on a diet. I'm only helping you."

"Excuse me?! What's that got to do with this, huh?!"

"I see no one's going to leave any tuna for me! You should show more appreciation for the chef!"

"Shiika, here, have another piece."

"*Nom*... Mm, delicious."

"What are you doing, you gluttonous siblings?! There's none left!"

Team Name: Ryouran High Music Department (Working Title)

Members
Gakuto Ikebukuro. Impachi Live Subscribers: 0 (No account registered.)
Shiika Ikebukuro. Impachi Live Subscribers: 36,400
Mana Akihabara. Impachi Live Subscribers: 8,800
Erio Shibuya. Impachi Live Subscribers: 502,700
Nokia Komae. Impachi Live Subscribers: 185,000

A colossal force that would shake all the students of Ryouran High to their very cores was born.

The launch of this team would rouse the interest and fighting spirit of all the talented students in the school and would eventually serve as the catalyst for a huge change involving both the online streaming world and the entertainment industry.

But it was only later that we would come to realize that.

To be continued...

MV Available Now!
Omn
Producer
Q-MHz
Vocalist
Tomori Kusunoki
Illustrator
necömi

idirectional Lost Ones Catalog

Fantasia Bunko

Afterword

Hello, I'm the author, Ghost Mikawa. Thank you for picking up a copy of *Looks Are All You Need*. This is my first time working with Fujimi Fantasia Bunko. Greetings to all Fantasia readers. And hello again to readers who've read my work from other labels, too.

Now then, I'd like to talk a little about the story of *Looks Are All You Need*, so if you haven't finished reading yet, please return to the page you were last on. Please read this afterword at your leisure once you're done, okay?

...All right. Now then, I'll discuss a bit about this volume.

First off, although the title is *Looks Are All You Need*, I'm certainly not trying to push the values this title might indicate onto others. I personally believe there isn't a gold standard for what determines good looks or bad looks, nor am I stating the entertainment industry or other industries is or should be influenced solely by physical appearances... But it's for this reason that I chose this kind of world as the backdrop for the character of Shiika and her brother.

At the same time, I don't discount the importance of looks altogether. The importance of visual presentation... Well, I'd like to explore this subject from all directions and all possible angles. This is just my conjecture, but hopefully it will resonate with one or two people out there.

Complex issues aside, I also simply wanted to have a sort of socially inept, nonexpressive heroine who needs to be looked after. Just picturing Shiika being cared for by Gakuto, it's like taking a supplement to instantly boost one's mood. Super fun.

Here are the acknowledgments.

The illustrator, necömi. Thank you for the wonderful illustrations! All the characters, including Shiika and Gakuto, are completely charming. I always looked forward to receiving new designs and illustrations. In particular, the cover is so beautiful that it makes me want to hang it up in my home. Thank you very much. I'll do my best to make this series popular, so I hope we can continue to enjoy working together. Thank you for your continued support!

Everyone at Q-MHz, thank you for creating a wonderful song for the original MV project of this novel. I was surprised to discover how much work goes into making a single song. The finished piece, "Omnidirectional Lost Ones Catalog," was wonderful, and I personally have listened to it many times (ha-ha). I'm so grateful for your patience and cooperation, although I'm sure there was a lot that I didn't understand because of my lack of experience. Thank you for your continued support!

To the vocalist, Tomori Kusunoki. It's a very difficult song to sing, so I was excited to see how it would turn out, but your singing voice was even more spectacular than I imagined. You combined the charisma of Shiika, a prodigious vocalist, with a faint hint of edginess, and I'm really looking forward to having the readers all listen to it. Thank you so much. And thank you for your continued support!

Writers and friends, Bisui Takahashi, Ryu Hirosaki, and Miya. Thank you for helping me with your knowledge of music, entertainment, streaming, and so on!

In addition, M (whose real name won't be used at their request) allowed me to interview them about the music and entertainment industry, dance, and many other aspects of its culture that I needed in order to write this book. This work would not have been completed without the cooperation of M, so thank you very much.

To the two editors in charge, S and S (both with the same initial!): Thank you for encouraging this project about the entertainment world, completely out of nowhere. This novel was able to see the light of day thanks to you. I'm sorry for the inconvenience caused during the writing of the manuscript, but I hope you will both stick with me in the future as well!

Thank you to everyone who has contributed to the publication of this novel. I am always indebted to you, and it's not just this time around, either. Simply writing a novel isn't enough to get it published and into the hands of the readers, and I believe that I am only able to call myself a writer due to the assistance of those around me. Thank you very much!

And finally, dear readers. Thank you for picking up *Looks Are All You Need* and reading until the end! I'm still envisioning many future stories about the prodigious talent known as Shiika, so I'd be happy if you would be so kind as to stick with this series for the long haul.

The beginning of a new story is always exciting. I will do my best to write as long, deep, and in-depth a saga as possible, so please continue to support me. Ghost Mikawa, signing off.